DOVER · THRIFT · EDITIONS

The Metamorphosis and Other Stories

FRANZ KAFKA

Translated by Stanley Appelbaum

DOVER PUBLICATIONS, INC.
New York

DOVER THRIFT EDITIONS

General Editor: Stanley Appelbaum

Copyright

Bibliographical Note

The present edition, first published by Dover Publications, Inc., in 1996, consists of new English translations of five stories by Kafka, translated from standard German editions. (See the Contents page for data on the original German publications.) The translation of "The Judgment" has already appeared in the 1993 Dover volume *Five Great German Short Stories/Fünf deutsche Meistererzählungen: A Dual-Language Book*, translated and edited by Stanley Appelbaum. The other four translations, also by Appelbaum, have never appeared elsewhere. A new Note has been written specially for the present volume.

Library of Congress Cataloging-in-Publication Data

Kafka, Franz, 1883–1924.
    [Short stories. English. Selections]
    The metamorphosis and other stories / Franz Kafka ; translated by Stanley Appelbaum.
       p.   cm. — (Dover thrift editions)
    Contents: The judgment — The metamorphosis — In the penal colony — A country doctor — A report to an academy.
    ISBN 0-486-29030-1 (pbk.)
    1. Kafka, Franz, 1883–1924—Translations into English.   I. Appelbaum, Stanley.
II. Title. III. Series.
PT2621.A26A277   1995
833'.912—dc20   95-20498
                                          CIP

Manufactured in the United States of America
Dover Publications, Inc., 31 East 2nd Street, Mineola, N.Y. 11501

Note

BY CHANNELING HIS own most personal inhibitions, anxieties and fantasies into highly imaginative stories and novels that were far ahead of their time, Franz Kafka (1883–1924) became a universal spokesman for perplexed and frightened twentieth-century man. He transcended the status of all the minorities he belonged to: as a resident of Prague, an exploited outpost of the Austro-Hungarian Empire; as a member of the German-speaking community within Bohemian-speaking Prague (an articulate artistic community that also included Rilke, Werfel and Meyrink); as a Jew among the German speakers; and (though far from asocial) as a total individualist among the Jews.

The five stories newly translated here were written during one of Kafka's peak periods; all were published in his lifetime in authoritative versions. (See the table of contents for dates of composition and publication.) Each of these stories is fully representative of various facets of his thought, his chief themes and genres, his constant obsessions.

"The Judgment" was the first of Kafka's stories that completely satisfied his own high demands and convinced him that he ought to go on writing (as a psychologically indispensable spare-time avocation; he held full-time jobs with insurance companies). The inferiority complex that his powerful, coarse-grained father had instilled in sickly Franz since childhood is reflected in the conflict between Georg Bendemann and Bendemann senior in the story. The protagonist's surname is modeled indirectly on Kafka's own, and the name Frieda Brandenfeld is modeled on that of Kafka's own fiancée at the time (none of his engagements ever ended in marriage).

Another son who is "punished" for mysterious reasons is Gregor Samsa (this surname is even closer to the author's) in "The Metamorphosis." Gregor's apartment and living arrangements are very similar to Kafka's own at the time of writing. The careful accumulation of verisimilitudinous everyday details and the circumstantial, "Talmudi-cal" reasoning of the main character — all within a situation that is impossible a priori — are recurring features of Kafka's work, as is the well-balanced coexistence of detached humor and deep-seated horror. Kafka's sympathetic portrayal of the trials of a petty bourgeois worker should not go unnoticed, either.

A third story of punishment is "In the Penal Colony," which may just possibly have the broadest ramifications of all those collected here. Immediately obvious are the vein of raw cruelty and the ultra-black humor, but a social theme is also touched on in the contrast between the governor's palace complex and the wretched conditions outside it; a political theme in the frightening forecast of totalitarian thought pat-terns and the slow crumbling of the machinery of government; and, almost surely, a religious and eschatological theme in the significance of the mechanized sacrifice and the prophecy that the old governor will return from the dead.

It is impossible to read "A Country Doctor," a breathless, all-in-one-paragraph nightmare vision, without recalling not only Kafka's visits to his own country-doctor uncle, with his onerous, never-ending rounds, but also Kafka's own "fine wound," the tuberculosis that would carry him off in just a few years more.

The very witty "A Report to an Academy" combines at least three of Kafka's favorite themes: animals endowed with human reasoning powers though otherwise bound by their own natural physique and habits ("The Metamorphosis" falls within this category, too); the psy-chological examination of the state of captivity; and the vaudeville or circus performer as a representative of the exposed and lonely life of the creative artist in society.

These new translations, in idiomatic modern American English, attempt to be more complete and correct than the old British versions, in which outright errors sometimes cloud the meaning to a serious degree, slight omissions occur, idioms are misunderstood, and Kafka's humor is often negated by pallid paraphrases of wording that is very sprightly in the original German.

Contents

The Judgment

IT WAS ON a Sunday morning in the loveliest part of the spring. Georg Bendemann, a young merchant, sat in his room on the second floor of one of the low, lightly built houses that extended along the river in a long line, differing, if at all, only in height and coloration. He had just finished a letter to a childhood friend who was living abroad; he sealed the letter with playful slowness and then, leaning his elbow on the desk, looked out the window at the river, the bridge and the pale-green hills on the far bank.

He thought about how this friend, dissatisfied with his advancement at home, had, years ago now, literally fled to Russia. Now this friend was running a business in St. Petersburg that had been very promising at the start, but for a long time now seemed to be at a standstill, as he complained during his increasingly infrequent visits to Georg. And so he was wearing himself out uselessly far from home; his foreign-style beard failed to disguise the face Georg had known so well since they were children, a face whose yellow complexion was apparently the sign of a developing illness. As he told Georg, he had no close relations with the colony of his compatriots in that place, but, in addition, practically no social intercourse with native families, and thus was in a fair way to remain a bachelor always.

What was one to write to a man like that, who had obviously taken a wrong course, whom one could pity but not help? Should one perhaps advise him to come home, resume his life back here, restore all his old friendships (there was no obstacle to this) and, for all the rest, rely on his friends' assistance? But that would mean nothing less than to tell him at the same time — hurting him more, the more one wished to spare his feelings — that his efforts up to now had been unsuccessful, that he should finally abandon them, that he had to return and be gaped at by everyone as a man who had come back as a failure. It would mean

1

telling him that his friends were the only ones with any sense, and that he was just a grown-up child who should merely obey his successful friends that had stayed at home. And was it even certain that all the pain that would have to be inflicted on him would be to any purpose? Maybe they wouldn't even succeed in bringing him home at all—for he himself said that he no longer understood the conditions back home— and so he would remain abroad in spite of everything, embittered by their suggestions and all the more alienated from his friends. But if he actually followed their advice and were to come to grief here—not intentionally, of course, but through circumstances—if he failed to find a proper footing either with or without his friends, if he suffered humiliation, if he then really had no home or friends left, wasn't it much better for him to remain abroad just as he was? In such circumstances, was it possible to believe that he would actually make a go of it here?

For these reasons, if one was to maintain communication by letter at all, one could not send him any real news, as one would unhesitatingly do even to the most casual acquaintances. Now, it was more than three years since Georg's friend had been home, giving as a quite flimsy excuse for his absence the instability of political conditions in Russia, which according to him did not allow a small businessman to leave his work for even the briefest period—while hundreds of thousands of Russians were calmly traveling all over. In the course of those three years, however, much had changed for Georg in particular. The death of Georg's mother, which had occurred about two years earlier, since which time Georg had been sharing the household with his old father, had, of course, still been communicated to his friend. The friend had expressed his sympathy in a letter so dry that the only possible explanation for it was that mourning over such an event becomes quite unimaginable when one is abroad. But, in addition, since that time Georg had taken charge of the family business with greater decisiveness, as he had done with everything else. Perhaps, while his mother was alive, his father had hindered Georg from taking a really active part in the business by insisting that only *his* views were valid; perhaps, since the death of Georg's mother, his father, while still working in the business, had become more withdrawn; perhaps—and this was extremely probable—lucky accidents played a far more important role. But at any rate, in these two years the business had grown at a quite unexpected rate, they had had to double their personnel, the returns had increased fivefold, and further expansion was undoubtedly due in the future.

But Georg's friend had no idea of this change. Earlier, perhaps most recently in that letter of sympathy, he had tried to persuade Georg to emigrate to Russia and had expatiated on the prospects in St. Petersburg for Georg's line of business in particular. The figures he quoted were infinitesimal compared with the volume of business Georg was now doing. But Georg had not felt like writing his friend about his business successes, and if he were to have done so belatedly now, it would really have looked odd.

And so Georg confined himself to continually writing his friend about nothing but insignificant events, as they accumulate disorderedly in one's memory when one thinks back on a quiet Sunday. His only wish was to leave undisturbed the mental picture of his hometown that his friend must have created during the long interval, a picture he could live with. And so it happened that three times, in letters written fairly far apart, Georg informed his friend of the engagement of a man of no consequence to an equally inconsequential girl, until his friend, quite contrary to Georg's intentions, really began to be interested in this curious fact.

But Georg far preferred to write him about things like that than to admit that he himself, a month earlier, had become engaged to a Miss Frieda Brandenfeld, a girl from a well-to-do family. He often spoke to his fiancée about that friend and their special relationship as correspondents. "Now, he won't come to our wedding," she said, "and I do have the right to meet all your friends." "I don't want to bother him," Georg replied; "mind you, he probably would come — at least, I think so — but he would feel constrained and injured; perhaps he would envy me, and he would surely go back again alone, discontented and incapable of ever overcoming that discontentment. Alone — do you know what that means?" "Yes, but couldn't he come to hear about our marriage in some other way?" "Naturally I can't prevent that, but, given his mode of life, it's not likely." "If you have friends like that, Georg, you shouldn't have become engaged at all." "Yes, that's the fault of both of us; but even so I wouldn't have wanted it any other way." And when she then, breathing rapidly as he kissed her, still managed to say: "And yet it does really make me sad," he decided it would really do no harm to write his friend about everything. "That's how I am and that's how he's got to accept me," he said to himself; "I can't remake myself into a person who might be more suited to be his friend than I am."

And, in fact, in the long letter he composed on that Sunday morning he informed his friend of the engagement that had taken place, writing as follows: "I have saved the best news for the end. I have become engaged to a Miss Frieda Brandenfeld, a girl from a well-to-do family that did not move here until long after your departure, and whom you thus can hardly be expected to know. There will be further opportunities to tell you details about my fiancée; let it suffice for today that I am very happy and that the only change in the relationship between you and me is that, in place of a very ordinary friend, you will now have in me a happy friend. In addition, in my fiancée, who sends warmest regards and who will soon write to you herself, you are acquiring a sincere female friend, which is not totally insignificant for a bachelor. I know that all sorts of things prevent you from visiting us, but wouldn't my wedding, of all things, be the right occasion for you to cast all obstacles to the winds? However that may be, though, don't make any special allowances but act only as you see fit."

With this letter in his hand Georg had sat at his desk for a long time, his face turned toward the window. When an acquaintance had greeted him from the street passing by, he had barely responded with an absent smile.

Finally he put the letter in his pocket and stepped from his room across a small corridor into his father's room, which he had not been in for months. Nor was there any particular need for him to go there, because he saw his father constantly in their office and they took their lunch in a restaurant at the same hour; in the evening, to be sure, each of them saw to his own needs as he wished, but then usually (unless Georg, as happened most often, was together with friends or, as things were now, visited his fiancée) each would sit with his newspaper for another little while in the living room that they shared.

Georg was surprised at how dark his father's room was even on this sunny morning. So the high wall that rose beyond the narrow yard cast such a great shadow! His father was sitting by the window in a corner that was decorated with various mementos of his late mother, and was reading the newspaper, which he held off to one side in front of his face, attempting to correct some eye condition. On the table were the leftovers of his breakfast, not much of which seemed to have been eaten.

"Ah, Georg!" said his father and walked right over to him. His heavy bathrobe opened as he walked, the tails flapping around him — "My father is *still* a giant," Georg said to himself.

"But it's unbearably dark here," he said then.

"Yes, it is dark, isn't it?" his father answered.

"You shut the window, too?"

"I like it better this way."

"But it's quite warm outside," said Georg, as an addition to his earlier remark, and sat down.

His father cleared away the breakfast dishes and put them on a chest.

"All that I really wanted to tell you," continued Georg, who was following the old man's movements in great perplexity, "is that, after all,

I have written to St. Petersburg announcing my engagement." He drew the letter a little way out of his pocket and let it slide back.

"What do you mean, to St. Petersburg?" asked his father.

"To my friend, of course," said Georg and tried to meet his father's eyes. — "At work he's quite different," he thought; "the way he sits here, filling out the chair, with his arms folded over his chest!"

"Yes. To your friend," said his father with a special emphasis.

"You know, of course, Father, that at first I wanted to keep my engagement a secret from him. Out of consideration for his feelings, for no other reason. You know yourself, he's a difficult man. I said to myself that he could find out about my engagement in some other way, even though, given his lonely way of life, that's hardly likely — I couldn't prevent that — but that he definitely wasn't going to find out about it from me."

"And now you've changed your mind?" asked his father, laid his voluminous paper down on the windowsill and put his glasses, which he covered with his hand, on top of the paper.

"Yes, now I have changed my mind. If he is a good friend of mine, I said to myself, then my happy engagement is a bit of happiness for him too. And therefore I no longer hesitated to tell him about it. But before I mailed the letter I wanted to tell you."

"Georg," said his father and drew the corners of his toothless mouth out wide, "listen! You came to me with this matter to consult with me. That doubtless does you honor. But it is meaningless, it is worse than meaningless, if you don't tell me the whole truth now. I don't wish to stir up matters that don't pertain to this. Since the death of your dear mother, certain unpleasant things have occurred. Perhaps the time is coming for them, too, and perhaps it is coming sooner than we think. At work a lot escapes me; perhaps it isn't intentionally hidden from me — for the moment I shall definitely assume that it is not hidden from me — I am no longer strong enough, my memory is going, I can no longer keep up with all the particulars. For one thing, that is perfectly natural for my age, and, for another, your mother's death took a much greater toll of me than of you. — But since we are discussing this matter, this letter, I implore you, Georg, don't deceive me. It's a trifle, it's not worth mentioning, so don't deceive me. Do you really have this friend in St. Petersburg?"

Georg stood up in embarrassment. "Let's forget about my friends. A thousand friends are no substitute for my father. Do you know what I think? You don't take good enough care of yourself. But old age demands its due. I can't do without you in the business, you know that very well, but if the business were to threaten your health, I would shut it down forever tomorrow. This is no good. We must institute a new way of life for you. And thoroughly. You sit here in the dark while you would have fine light in the living room. You nibble at your breakfast instead of nourishing yourself properly. You sit by a closed window while the air would do you so much good. No, Father! I am going to get the doctor and we'll follow his advice. We'll exchange rooms; you'll move into the front room, I'll move in here. It won't mean any change for you, all your possessions will be brought in with you. But there's time for all that; for the moment do lie down in bed for a while, you definitely need rest. Come, I'll help you undress; you'll see, I can. Or if you want to go to the front room at once, then you can lie down on my bed for the time being. In fact, that would be very sensible."

Georg was standing close by his father, who had let his head, with its disheveled white hair, drop onto his breast.

"Georg," said his father quietly, without moving.

Georg immediately knelt down beside his father; in his father's weary face he saw that the unnaturally large pupils in the corners of the eyes were directed at himself.

"You have no friend in St. Petersburg. You've always been a practical joker and you haven't spared even me. How could you have a friend there, of all places! I can't believe that at all."

"Just try to remember, Father," said Georg, lifting his father from the armchair and drawing off his bathrobe as the old man now stood there in great debility; "it's now almost three years ago that my friend was here on a visit. I still recall that you didn't particularly like him. At least twice I told you that he wasn't here, although he was sitting in my room at the moment. Of course, I could understand your dislike of him very well: my friend does have his peculiarities. But then after all you got along very well with him again. I was still so proud at the time that you listened to him, nodded and asked him questions. If you think about it, you must remember. At the time he told us unbelievable stories about the Russian revolution. For example, how, on a business trip to Kiev, during a riot he had seen a priest on a balcony cutting a wide bloody cross into the palm of his hand, raising that hand and addressing the crowd. You yourself repeated that story from time to time."

Meanwhile Georg had succeeded in sitting his father down again and carefully pulling off the long knitted drawers he wore over his linen underpants, as well as his socks. At sight of the not especially clean underwear, he reproached himself for having neglected his father. It surely would also have been his duty to watch over his father's changes of underwear. He had not yet spoken expressly with his fiancée about how they wished to arrange his father's future, for they had tacitly presupposed that his father would remain alone in the old house. But now he quickly decided, with full determination, to take his father along into his future household. Indeed, it almost seemed, upon examining the situation more closely, that the care that would be given his father there might come too late.

He carried his father to bed in his arms. He had a frightening feeling when he noticed, during the few paces over to the bed, that his father was playing with the watch chain on his chest. He couldn't put him right into bed because he was holding onto that watch chain so tightly.

But scarcely was he in bed when all seemed well. He covered himself and then pulled the blanket extremely far up over his shoulders. He looked up at Georg in a not unfriendly way.

"Then, you remember him now?" asked Georg and nodded to him encouragingly.

"Am I completely covered up now?" asked his father, as if he couldn't see whether his feet were sufficiently covered.

"So you're already pleased to be in bed," said Georg and tucked him in more thoroughly.

"Am I completely covered up?" asked his father again, and seemed to wait for the answer with particular attention.

"Relax, you're all covered up."

"No!" shouted his father, running his reply into his preceding remark, then threw the blanket back with such force that it completely unfolded for a moment as it flew through the air, and stood upright on the bed. He merely touched the ceiling lightly with one hand. "You wanted to cover me up, I know, offspring of mine, but I'm not covered up yet. And even if I am doing this with my last strength, it is enough for you — too much for you. Of course I know your friend. He would have been a son after my own heart. And that's why you have cheated him all these years. Why else? Do you think I haven't wept over him? Isn't that why you lock yourself into your office, so no one will disturb you — 'the boss is busy' — just so you can write your treacherous little letters to Russia. But fortunately no one needs to teach a father how to see through his son. Now that you believed you had got the better of him, got the better of him to such an extent that you can seat yourself on him with your backside and he won't move, this fine son of mine has decided to get married!"

Georg looked up at the frightening image his father presented. His St. Petersburg friend, whom his father suddenly knew so well, stirred his emotions as never before. He saw him lost in far-off Russia. He saw him at the door of his empty, plundered establishment. He was still standing amid the ruins of the shelves, the mangled merchandise, the falling gas brackets. Why did he have to travel so far away!

"But look at me!" shouted his father, and Georg ran almost absent-mindedly toward the bed, in order to grasp everything, but came to a sudden halt midway.

"Because she lifted her skirts," his father began to pipe, "because she lifted her skirts that way, the disgusting ninny," and, in order to depict this, he lifted his nightshirt so high that the scar from his war years could be seen on his upper thigh; "because she lifted her skirts so and so and so, you went for her, and in order to satisfy yourself with her without being disturbed, you profaned your mother's memory, betrayed your friend and stuck your father in bed so he couldn't move. But can he move or can't he?"

And he stood completely unsupported and flung out his legs. He was radiant with insight.

Georg stood in a corner, as far from his father as possible. A long time ago he had firmly decided to observe everything with complete thoroughness, so that he might not be somehow taken by surprise in a roundabout way, from behind, from above. Now he once more remembered that long-forgotten decision and forgot it, as one draws a short thread through the eye of a needle.

"But my friend is *not* betrayed!" shouted his father, and his index finger, moving to and fro, confirmed this. "I was his local representative here."

"Play actor!" Georg could not help calling out, immediately recognized the harm he had done himself, and, with staring eyes — but too late — bit his tongue so hard that he doubled up with pain.

"Yes, of course I was playing a part! Play actor! What a good expression! What other comfort remained for an old, bereaved father? Tell me — and, for the moment that it takes you to reply, be my living son yet — what else could I do, in my back room, persecuted by my faithless staff, old to my very bones? And my son went everywhere exultantly, closed business deals that I had set up, turned somersaults from joy, and moved about in front of his father with the poker face of a man of honor! Do you think I wouldn't have loved you, I who gave you your being?"

"Now he'll lean forward," thought Georg; "if he would only fall and smash himself!" This sentence hissed through his mind.

His father leaned forward, but did not fall. Since Georg did not come closer, as he had expected, he straightened up again.

"Stay where you are, I don't need you! You think you still have the strength to come over here, and are merely hanging back because you want to. Don't make a mistake! I am still by far the stronger. On my own I might have had to retreat, but your mother passed her strength along to me, I made a wonderful alliance with your friend, I have your clientele here in my pocket!"

"He even has pockets in his nightshirt!" Georg said to himself, and thought that he could obliterate him with that remark. He thought so only for a moment, because he kept forgetting everything.

"Just lock arms with your fiancée and come over to me. I'll sweep her away from your side before you know it!"

Georg made grimaces as if he didn't believe that. His father merely nodded toward Georg's corner, in asseveration of the truth of what he said.

"How you did amuse me today when you came and asked whether you should write your friend about your engagement. He knows everything, foolish boy, he knows everything! I wrote to him because you forgot to take away my writing supplies. That's why he hasn't come for years now, he knows everything a hundred times better than you do; he crumples up your letters in his left hand without reading them, while he holds my letters in front of him in his right hand to read them!"

In his enthusiasm he swung his arm above his head. "He knows everything a thousand times better!" he shouted.

"Ten thousand times!" said Georg, meaning to mock his father, but while still on his lips the words took on a deadly serious tone.

"For years I've been watching and waiting for you to come along with that question! Do you think I care about anything else? Do you think I read newspapers? There!" and he threw over to Georg a sheet of the newspaper that had somehow been carried into the bed along with him. An old paper, with a name now completely unknown to Georg.

"How long you hesitated before your time was ripe! Mother had to die, she couldn't live until the happy day; your friend is going to ruin in his Russia, even three years ago his face was yellow enough to throw away; and I—well, you see how things stand with me. That you have eyes for!"

"So you were lying in wait for me!" shouted Georg.

In a sympathetic tone his father said parenthetically: "You probably wanted to say that before. Now it's no longer fitting."

And in a louder voice: "So now you know what existed outside yourself; up to now you knew only about yourself! You were truly an innocent child, but even more truly you were a fiendish person! — And therefore know this: I now condemn you to death by drowning!"

Georg felt himself driven from the room; the crash with which his father collapsed onto the bed behind him was still in his ears as he went. On the staircase, as he dashed down the steps as if down an inclined plane, he knocked over his maid, who was about to go upstairs to tidy up the house after the night. "Jesus!" she cried and covered her face with her apron, but he was already gone. He leapt past the gate and across the roadway, impelled to reach the water. Now he clutched the railing as a hungry man clutches food. He vaulted over like the accomplished gymnast he had been in his youth, to his parents' pride. He was still holding tight with hands that were growing weaker; between the bars of the railing he caught sight of a bus that would easily smother the noise of his fall; he called softly: "Dear parents, I *did* always love you," and let himself fall.

At that moment a simply endless stream of traffic was passing over the bridge.

The Metamorphosis

I

WHEN GREGOR SAMSA awoke from troubled dreams one morning, he found that he had been transformed in his bed into an enormous bug. He lay on his back, which was hard as armor, and, when he lifted his head a little, he saw his belly — rounded, brown, partitioned by archlike ridges — on top of which the blanket, ready to slip off altogether, was just barely perched. His numerous legs, pitifully thin in comparison to the rest of his girth, flickered helplessly before his eyes.

"What's happened to me?" he thought. It was no dream. His room, a real room meant for human habitation, though a little too small, lay peacefully within its four familiar walls. Above the table, on which an unpacked sampling of fabric swatches was strewn — Samsa was a traveling salesman — hung the picture that he had recently cut out of an illustrated magazine and had placed in a pretty gilt frame. It depicted a lady who, decked out in a fur hat and a fur boa, sat upright, raising toward the viewer a heavy fur muff in which her whole forearm was encased.

Gregor's gaze then turned toward the window, and the dismal weather — you could hear raindrops beating against the window gutter — made him quite melancholy. "What if I went back to sleep for another while and forgot all this foolishness?" he thought; but that was totally out of the question, because he was used to sleeping on his right side, and in his present state he couldn't get into that position. No matter how energetically he threw himself onto his right side, each time he rocked back into the supine position. He must have tried a hundred times, closing his eyes to avoid seeing his squirming legs, not stopping until he began to feel a slight, dull pain in his side that he had never felt before.

"My God," he thought, "what a strenuous profession I've chosen! Traveling day in and day out. The turmoil of business is much greater than in the home office, and on top of that I'm subjected to this torment of traveling, to the worries about train connections, the bad meals at

11

irregular hours, an intercourse with people that constantly changes, never lasts, never becomes cordial. The devil take it all!" He felt a slight itch up on his belly; slowly shoved himself on his back closer to the bedpost, so he could lift his head better; found the itchy place, which was all covered with little white spots that he was unable to diagnose; and wanted to feel the area with one leg, but drew it back immediately, because when he touched it he was invaded by chills.

He slid back into his former position. "Getting up early like this," he thought, "makes you totally idiotic. People must have their sleep. Other traveling salesmen live like harem women. For instance, when during the course of the morning I go back to the hotel to copy out the orders I've received, those fine gentlemen are just having their breakfast. I should try that with my boss; I'd be fired on the spot. Anyway, who knows whether that wouldn't be a good thing for me after all. If I didn't hold myself back because of my parents, I would have quit long ago; I would have walked right up to the boss and let my heart out to him. He would surely have fallen off his desk! That's a peculiar habit of his, too, sitting on his desk and talking down to his employees from up above; and, besides, they have to step way up close because the boss is so hard of hearing. Now, I haven't given up all hope yet; once I have the money together to pay off my parents' debt to him — that should still take five or six years — I'll definitely go through with it. Then I'll make the big break. At the moment, of course, I've got to get up, because my train leaves at five."

And he glanced over toward his alarm clock, which was ticking on the wardrobe. "Father in Heaven!" he thought. It was half past six, and the hands were moving ahead peacefully; in fact, it was later than half past, it was almost a quarter to seven. Could the alarm have failed to ring? From the bed he could see that it was correctly set for four; surely, it had also rung. Yes, but was it possible to sleep peacefully through that furniture-shaking ring? Well, he hadn't slept peacefully, but probably all the more soundly for that. Yet, what should he do now? The next train left at seven; to catch it he would have had to make a mad dash, his sample case wasn't packed yet, and he himself definitely didn't feel particularly fresh and lively. And even if he caught the train, he couldn't escape a bawling out from his boss, because the office messenger had waited at the five-o'clock train and had long since made a report about his negligence. He was a creature of the boss's, spineless and stupid. Now, what if he reported in sick? But that would be extremely distressing and suspicious, because during his five years' employment Gregor had not been ill even once. The boss would surely arrive with the health-insurance doctor, would complain to his parents about their lazy son and would cut short all objections by referring them to the health-insurance doctor, in whose eyes the only people that exist at all are perfectly healthy specimens who are work-shy. And besides, would he be so wrong in this case? Actually, aside from a truly excessive drowsiness after all that sleep, Gregor felt quite well and in fact was particularly hungry.

While he was considering all this in the greatest haste, still unable to decide whether to get out of bed—the clock was just striking six forty-five—there was a cautious knock on the door at the head of his bed. "Gregor," a voice called—it was his mother—"it's six forty-five. Didn't you intend to make a trip?" That gentle voice! Gregor was frightened when he heard his own answering voice, which, to be sure, was unmistakably his accustomed one, but in which there now appeared, as if rising from below, an irrepressible, painful peeping sound, so that his words retained their clarity only at the very outset but became distorted as they faded away, so that you couldn't tell if you had heard them correctly. Gregor had meant to give a detailed answer and explain everything, but under the circumstances he merely said: "Yes, yes; thanks, Mother; I'm getting up now." Because the door was made of wood, the alteration in Gregor's voice was probably not noticeable, since his mother was pacified by that explanation and shuffled away. But as a result of that brief conversation the other members of the family had become aware that, contrary to expectation, Gregor was still at home; and his father was soon knocking at one of the side doors, softly, but with his fist. "Gregor, Gregor," he called, "what's going on?" And before very long he admonished him again, in a deeper voice: "Gregor! Gregor!" But at the other side door his sister was quietly lamenting: "Gregor? Aren't you well? Do you need anything?" Gregor answered in both directions: "Be right there!" He made an effort, by enunciating most carefully and by inserting long pauses between the individual words, to free his voice of anything out of the ordinary. His father then returned to his breakfast, but his sister whispered: "Gregor, open up, I beg you." But Gregor had not the slightest intention of opening the door; in fact, he was now glad he had formed the cautious habit, an offshoot of his business trips, of locking all his doors at night even at home.

First he wanted to get up in peace and unmolested, get dressed and, especially, have breakfast, and only afterwards give the matter further thought, because, as he now realized, in bed he would never arrive at any sensible conclusion to his musings. He recalled that, often in the past, while in bed, he had felt some slight pain or other, perhaps caused by lying in an awkward position, and that, when he got out of bed, the pain had proved to be purely imaginary; and he was eager to find out how his impressions of that morning would gradually be dispelled. That the alteration in his voice was nothing more than the harbinger of a nasty cold, a professional hazard of traveling salesmen, he had not the slightest doubt.

To throw off the blanket was quite easy; all he needed to do was puff himself up a little and it fell down by itself. But after that things became difficult, especially since he was so unusually wide. He would normally have used his arms and hands to hoist himself up; but instead of them he now had only the numerous little legs, which were uninterruptedly moving in the most confused way and which, in addition, he couldn't control. Whenever he intended to bend one of them, at first he extended it; and when he finally succeeded in executing his wishes with that particular leg, all of the others meanwhile would thrash about as if they were completely independent, in an extreme, painful agitation. "But I can't stay in bed doing nothing," Gregor said to himself.

First he wanted to leave the bed with the lower part of his body, but this lower part, which, by the way, he hadn't seen yet and of which he couldn't form any clear idea, either, proved to be too difficult to move around; the procedure was so slow; and when finally, having grown almost wild, he gathered all his strength and pushed forward heedlessly, he went in the wrong direction and collided violently with the lower bedpost. The burning pain that he felt taught him that it was precisely the lower part of his body that was perhaps the most sensitive at the moment.

Therefore, he tried to get the upper part of his body out of bed first, and carefully turned his head toward the edge of the bed. He managed to do this easily and, despite its width and weight, finally the bulk of his body slowly followed in the direction his head had turned. But when at last he had moved his head into the open space outside the bed, he became afraid of continuing to edge forward in this manner, because if he finally let himself fall like that, it would take a real miracle to keep his head from being injured. And now of all times he must take every precaution not to lose consciousness; rather than that, he would stay in bed.

But when once again, heaving a sigh after similar efforts, he lay there just as before, and once again saw his little legs battling one another even more pitifully, if that were possible — when he could find no possibility of bringing calm and order into that arbitrary turmoil — he told himself again that he couldn't possibly stay in bed, and that the most sensible thing was to make every sacrifice if there existed even the smallest hope of thereby freeing himself from bed. But at the same time he didn't forget to remind himself occasionally that the calmest possible reflection is far preferable to desperate decisions. At such moments he would direct his eyes as fixedly as possible toward the window, but unfortunately there was not much confidence or cheer to be derived from the sight of the morning fog, which even shrouded the other side of the narrow street. "Seven o'clock already," he said to himself as the clock struck again, "seven o'clock already and still such a fog." And for a little while he lay there calmly, breathing very gently, as if perhaps expecting the total silence to restore him to his real, understandable condition.

But then he said to himself: "Before it strikes seven fifteen, I just have to be all the way out of bed. Besides, by that time someone from the firm will come to ask about me, because the office opens before seven o'clock." And now he prepared to rock his entire body out of bed at its full length in a uniform movement. If he let himself fall out of bed in this manner, he expected that his head, which he intended to lift up high during the fall, would receive no injury. His back seemed to be hard; when falling onto the carpet, surely nothing would happen to it. His greatest fear was the thought of the loud crash which must certainly result, and which would probably cause, if not a scare, then at least concern on the other side of all the doors. But that risk had to be taken.

When Gregor was already projecting halfway out of bed — this new method was more of a game than a hard task, all he needed to do was keep on rocking back and forth in short spurts — it occurred to him how simple everything would be if someone came to help him. Two strong people — he thought of his father and the maid — would have completely sufficed; they would only have had to shove their arms under his rounded back, extract him from bed that way like a nut from its shell, stoop down under his bulk and then merely wait cautiously until he had swung himself entirely over on the floor, where hopefully his little legs would find their use. Now, completely apart from the fact that the doors were locked, should he really have called for help? Despite all his tribulations, he was unable to suppress a smile at that thought.

He had now proceeded so far that, when rocking more vigorously, he could barely still maintain his equilibrium, and would very soon have to reach a definitive decision, because in five minutes it would be seven fifteen — when there was a ring at the apartment door. "That's somebody from the firm," he said to himself and nearly became rigid, while his little legs danced all the more quickly. For a moment everything remained quiet. "They aren't opening," Gregor said to himself, enmeshed in some unreasoning hope. But then, naturally, just as always, the maid went to the door with a firm tread and opened it. Gregor needed only to hear the visitor's first words of greeting and he already knew who it was — the chief clerk himself. Why was only Gregor condemned to work for a firm where people immediately conceived the greatest suspicions at the smallest sign of negligence? Were all employees simply scoundrels, was there among them not one loyal, devoted person who, even though he had merely failed to utilize a couple of morning hours on behalf of the firm, had become crazed by pangs of conscience, to the point of being incapable of getting out of bed? Wouldn't it really have been enough to send an apprentice to ask — if all this questioning was necessary at all — did the chief clerk himself have to come, thereby indicating to the entire innocent family that the investigation into this suspicious incident could only be entrusted to the intelligence of the chief clerk? And, more as a result of the irritation that these reflections caused Gregor, than as a result of a proper decision, he swung himself out of bed with all his might. There was a loud thump, but it wasn't a real crash. The fall was deadened somewhat by the carpet, and in addition Gregor's back was more resilient than he had thought, so that the muffled sound wasn't so noticeable. But he hadn't held his head carefully enough and had bumped it; he turned it and rubbed it against the carpet in vexation and pain.

"Something fell in there," said the chief clerk in the room on the left side. Gregor tried to imagine whether the chief clerk might not some day have an experience similar to his of today: the possibility really had to be conceded. But, as if in brutal response to this question, the chief clerk now took a few determined steps in the adjoining room, which made his patent-leather boots squeak. From the room on the right side Gregor's sister whispered, to inform him: "Gregor, the chief clerk is here." "I know," said Gregor to himself, but he didn't dare to raise his voice so loud that his sister could hear him.

"Gregor," his father now said from the room on the left side, "the chief clerk has come and is inquiring why you didn't leave by the early train. We don't know what to tell him. Besides, he wants to talk with you personally. So please open the door. He will surely be kind enough to forgive the disorder in your room." "Good morning, Mr. Samsa," the chief clerk meanwhile called, in a friendly tone. "He isn't well," Gregor's mother said to the chief clerk while his father was still talking at the door, "he isn't well, believe me, sir. How otherwise would Gregor miss a train! The boy has no head for anything but the business. I'm almost upset, as it is, that he never goes out at night; he's been in town for eight days this time, but has stayed at home every night. He sits with us at the table and reads the paper quietly or studies timetables. It's already a distraction for him when he busies himself with fretsaw work. So, for example, during two or three evenings he carved a small frame; you'll be amazed how pretty it is; it's hanging in his room; you'll see it right away when Gregor opens up. Besides, I'm glad you're here, sir; on our own we couldn't have persuaded Gregor to open the door; he's so obstinate; and

I'm sure he's not feeling well, even though he denied it earlier this morning." "I'll be right there," said Gregor slowly and deliberately, but not making a move, so as to lose not a word of the conversation. "I, too, my dear lady, can think of no other explanation," said the chief clerk; "I hope it's nothing serious. Although I am also bound to state that we business people — unfortunately or fortunately, according to how you look at it — very often simply have to overcome a slight indisposition out of regard for the business." "Well, can the gentleman go in to see you now?" asked the impatient father, and knocked on the door again. "No," said Gregor. In the room on the left side a painful silence ensued, in the room on the right side the sister began to sob.

Why didn't the sister go and join the others? She had probably just gotten out of bed and hadn't even begun dressing. And why was she crying? Because he didn't get up and let the chief clerk in? Because he was in danger of losing his job, and because then his boss would once more dun their parents for his old claims? For the time being those were needless worries, after all. Gregor was still here and hadn't the slightest thought of abandoning his family. At the moment he was lying there on the carpet, and no one acquainted with his current state could seriously have asked him to let in the chief clerk. But, after all, Gregor couldn't really be discharged at once on account of this slight discourtesy, for which a suitable excuse would easily be found later on. And it seemed to Gregor that it would be much more sensible to leave him in peace for now instead of disturbing him with tears and exhortations. But it was precisely all the uncertainty that was oppressing the others and that excused their behavior.

"Mr. Samsa," the chief clerk now called in a louder voice, "what's going on? You're barricading yourself in your room, giving just 'yes' and 'no' answers, causing your parents big, needless worries and — to mention this just incidentally — neglecting your business duties in a truly unheard-of fashion. I am speaking here in the name of your parents and of your employer, and I am asking you quite seriously for an immediate, lucid explanation. I'm amazed, I'm amazed. I thought I knew you for a calm, sensible person, and now suddenly you apparently want to begin making an exhibition of peculiar caprices. To be sure, early this morning our employer, when speaking to me, hinted at a possible explanation for your negligence — it concerned the cash receipts that were recently entrusted to you — but, honestly, I all but gave him my word of honor that that explanation couldn't be the true one. Now, however, I see your incomprehensible stubbornness here and I am losing all willingness to say a good word for you in the slightest way. Nor is your position by any means the most solid. I originally had the intention of telling you all this between ourselves, but since you are making me waste my time here pointlessly, I don't know why your parents shouldn't hear it, too. Well, then, your performance recently has been most unsatisfactory; true, this isn't the season for doing especially good business, we acknowledge that; but a season for doing no business at all just doesn't exist, Mr. Samsa, it can't be allowed to exist." "But, sir," Gregor called out in distraction, forgetting everything else in his excitement, "I'm going to open the door immediately, this minute. A slight indisposition, a dizzy spell, have prevented me from getting up. I'm still lying in bed. But now I feel quite lively again. I am just now climbing out of bed. Be patient for just another moment! I'm not quite as well yet as I thought. But I now feel all right. The things that can affect a person! Just last evening I felt perfectly fine, my parents know that; or it might be better to say that even last evening I had a little advance indication. People should have noticed it from the way I looked. Why didn't I report it at the office?! But you always think that you'll be able to fight off an illness without having to stay home. Sir! Spare my parents! There is no basis for all the complaints you're now making against me; and no one has said a word to me about them. Perhaps you haven't read the last orders I sent in. Besides, I'll still make the trip on the eight-o'clock train, the couple of hours of rest have strengthened me. Don't waste your time here, sir; I'll be at the office myself in no time, and please be good enough to tell them that and give my best wishes to our employer!"

And while Gregor was pouring all of this out hastily, scarcely knowing what he was saying, he had approached the wardrobe without difficulty, probably because of the practice he had already had in bed, and was now trying to draw himself up against it. He wanted actually to open the door, actually to show himself and speak with the chief clerk; he was eager to learn what the others, who were now so desirous of his presence, would say when they saw him. If they got frightened, then Gregor would have no further responsibility and could be calm. But if they accepted everything calmly, then he, too, would have no cause to be upset, and, if he hurried, he could really be at the station at eight o'clock. At first, now, he slid back down the smooth wardrobe several times, but finally, giving himself one last thrust, he stood there upright; he paid no more attention to the pains in his abdomen, severe as they were. Now he let himself fall against the backrest of a nearby chair and held tight to its edges with his little legs. By doing so, moreover, he had also gained control over himself and he fell silent, because now he could listen to the chief clerk.

"Did you understand even a single word?" the chief clerk was asking his parents; "he isn't trying to make a fool of us, is he?" "God forbid," called his mother, who was weeping by this time, "he may be seriously ill, and we're torturing him. Grete! Grete!" she then shouted. "Mother?" called his sister from the other side. They were communicating across Gregor's room. "You must go to the doctor's at once. Gregor is sick. Fetch the doctor fast. Did you hear Gregor speaking just now?" "That was an animal's voice," said the chief clerk, noticeably quietly in contrast to the mother's shouting. "Anna! Anna!" called the father through the hallway into the kitchen, clapping his hands, "get a locksmith right away!" And already the two girls were running down the hallway with rustling skirts — how had his sister gotten dressed so quickly? — and tore open the apartment door. There was no sound of the door closing; they had most likely left it open, as is the case in apartments where a great misfortune has occurred.

But Gregor had become much calmer. To be sure, he now realized that his speech was no longer intelligible, even though it had seemed clear enough to him, clearer than before, perhaps because his ears were getting used to it. But anyway they were now believing that there was something wrong with him and they were ready to help him. The confidence and security with which the first measures had been taken, comforted him. He felt that he was once more drawn into the circle of humanity and hoped for magnificent and surprising achievements on the part of both, the doctor and the locksmith, without really differentiating much between them. In order to restore his voice to its maximum clarity for the imminent decisive discussions, he cleared it a little by coughing, but took care to do this in very muffled tones, since possibly even that noise might sound different from human coughing, and he no longer trusted himself to make the distinction. Meanwhile it had become completely quiet in the adjoining room. Perhaps his parents were sitting at the table with the chief clerk and whispering quietly, perhaps they were all leaning against the door and listening.

Gregor shoved himself slowly to the door, using the chair; once there, he let it go and threw himself against the door, holding himself upright against it — the balls of his little feet contained some sticky substance — and rested there from his exertions for the space of a minute. But then he prepared to turn the key in the lock with his mouth. Unfortunately it seemed that he had no real teeth — what was he to grasp the key with? — but, instead, his jaws were actually pretty strong; with their help he did really get the key to move, paying no heed to the fact that he doubtless was doing himself some injury, because a brown fluid issued from his mouth, ran down over the key and dripped onto the floor. "Listen there," said the chief clerk in the adjoining room, "he's turning the key." That was a great encouragement for Gregor; but all of them should have called out to him, even his father and mother; "Go to it, Gregor!" they should have called, "keep at it, work on that lock!" And, imagining that they were all following his efforts in suspense, he bit recklessly into the key with all the strength he could muster. He danced around the lock, now here, now there, following the progress of the key as it turned; now he was keeping himself upright solely with his mouth, and, as the need arose, he either hung from the key or pushed it down again with the full weight of his body. The sharper sound of the lock, as it finally snapped back, woke Gregor up completely. With a sigh of relief he said to himself: "So then, I didn't need the locksmith," and he placed his head on the handle, in order to open the door all the way.

Since he had to open the door in this manner, he was still out of sight after it was already fairly wide open. First he had to turn his body slowly around one leaf of the double door, and very carefully at that, if he didn't want to fall squarely on his back right before entering the room. He was still occupied by that difficult maneuver and had no time to pay attention to anything else, when he heard the chief clerk utter a loud "Oh!"—it sounded like the wind howling—and now he saw him as well. He had been the closest to the door; now, pressing his hand against his open mouth, he stepped slowly backward as if driven away by some invisible force operating with uniform pressure. Gregor's mother—despite the presence of the chief clerk, she stood there with her hair still undone from the previous night and piled in a high, ruffled mass—first looked at his father with folded hands, then took two steps toward Gregor and collapsed in the midst of her petticoats, which billowed out all around her, her face completely lost to view and sunk on her chest. His father clenched his fist with a hostile expression, as if intending to push Gregor back into his room; then he looked around the parlor in uncertainty, shaded his eyes with his hands and wept so hard that it shook his powerful chest.

Gregor now refrained from entering the room; he stayed inside, leaning on the leaf of the door that was firmly latched, so that all that could be seen was half of his body and, above it, his head tilted to the side, with which he peered toward the others. Meanwhile it had become much brighter outside; clearly visible on the other side of the street was a section of the building situated opposite from them, endless, gray-black—it was a hospital—with its regularly placed windows harshly piercing its facade; the rain was still falling, but only in large drops that were individually visible and were literally flung down upon the ground one by one. An excessive number of breakfast dishes and utensils stood on the table, because for Gregor's father breakfast was the most important meal of the day and he would stretch it out for hours while reading a number of newspapers. On the wall precisely opposite hung a photograph of Gregor that dated from his military service, showing him as a lieutenant, hand on sword, with a carefree smile, demanding respect for his bearing and his uniform. The door to the hallway was open and, since the apartment door was open, too, there was a clear view all the way out onto the landing and the beginning of the downward staircase.

"Now," said Gregor, who was perfectly conscious of being the only one who had remained calm, "I'll get dressed right away, pack the sample case and catch the train. Is it all right, is it all right with you if I make the trip? Now, sir, you see that I'm not stubborn and I am glad to do my job; traveling is a nuisance, but without the traveling I couldn't live. Where are you off to, sir? To the office? Yes? Will you make an honest report of everything? There's a moment now and then when a man is incapable of working, but that's precisely the right moment to recall his past performance and to consider that, later on, when the obstacle is cleared away, he will surely work all the more diligently and with greater concentration. I am so deeply obligated to our employer, you know that very well. Besides, I have my parents and sister to worry about. I'm in a jam, but I'll work my way out of it. But don't make it harder for me than it already is. Speak up for me in the firm! A traveling salesman isn't well liked, I know. People think he makes a fortune and lives in clover. They have no particular reason to reflect on it and get over that prejudice. But you, sir, you have a better overview of the true state of affairs than the rest of the staff; in fact, speaking in all confidence, a better overview than our employer himself, who, in his role as entrepreneur, can easily be led to misjudge one of his employees. You are also well aware that a traveling salesman, who is away from the home office almost all year long, can thus easily fall victim to gossip, contingencies and groundless complaints that he's completely unable to defend himself against because he generally hears nothing about them; or else he finds out only when he has just come back from a trip, all worn out, and gets to feel the bad results at home, personally, when it's too late even to fathom the reasons for them. Sir, don't go away without saying a word to me that shows me that you agree with me even a little bit!"

But at Gregor's first words the chief clerk had already turned away, and only looked back at Gregor over his jerking shoulder, his lips pouting. And during Gregor's speech he didn't stand still for a minute, but, never losing sight of Gregor, retreated toward the door, very gradually, as if under a secret prohibition against leaving the room. By now he was in the hallway, and, from the abrupt movement with which he finally withdrew his foot from the parlor, anyone might think he had just burnt the sole of it. But in the hallway he stretched out his right hand as

far as it could go in the direction of the stairway, as if a truly superter-
restrial deliverance were awaiting him there.

Gregor realized that it simply wouldn't do to let the chief clerk depart
in that frame of mind, or else his position in the firm would be seriously
endangered. His parents didn't understand things like that so well: in all
those long years they had gained the conviction that Gregor was set up
for life in this firm, and, besides, they were now so preoccupied by the
troubles of the moment that they had lost track of all foresight. But
Gregor possessed that foresight. The chief clerk must be retained,
pacified, persuaded and finally won over; after all, the future of Gregor
and his family depended on it! If only his sister were here! She was
clever; she had already started to cry while Gregor was still lying calmly
on his back. And surely the chief clerk, who was an admirer of women,
would have let her manage him; she would have closed the parlor door
and talked him out of his fears in the hallway. But his sister *wasn't* there,
Gregor had to act on his own behalf. And without stopping to think that
he was still completely unfamiliar with his own present powers of
locomotion, without stopping to think that once again his oration had
possibly — in fact, probably — not been understood, he let go of the leaf
of the door; shoved himself through the opening; tried to reach the chief
clerk, who was already clutching the railing on the landing with both
hands in a ridiculous manner; but immediately, while seeking a support,
fell down onto his numerous legs with a brief cry. Scarcely had that
occurred when, for the first time that morning, he felt a sense of bodily
comfort; his little legs had solid ground below them; they obeyed
perfectly, as he noticed to his joy; in fact, they were eager to carry him
wherever he wanted to go; and he now believed that a definitive cure for
all his sorrow was immediately due. But at that very instant, rocking back
and forth as he contained his forward propulsion for a moment, he had
come very close to his mother, directly opposite her on the floor.
Suddenly she leaped up into the air, even though she had seemed so
totally lost to the world; she stretched out her arms wide, spread her
fingers and shouted: "Help, for the love of God, help!" She kept her
head lowered as if she wanted to get a better look at Gregor, but in
contradiction to that, she ran backwards recklessly. Forgetting that the
laid table was behind her, when she reached it she hastily sat down on it,
as if absentminded, and seemed not to notice that alongside her the
coffee was pouring onto the carpet in a thick stream out of the big
overturned pot.

"Mother, Mother," Gregor said softly, looking up at her. For a moment he had completely forgotten about the chief clerk; on the other
hand, seeing the flowing coffee, he couldn't resist snapping at the air

with his jaws a few times. This made his mother scream again, dash away from the table and fall into the arms of his father, who hastened to receive her. But now Gregor had no time for his parents; the chief clerk was already on the staircase; his chin on the railing, he was still looking back for a last time. Gregor spurted forward, to be as sure as possible of catching up with him; the chief clerk must have had some foreboding, because he made a jump down several steps and disappeared; but he was still shouting "Aaaah!"—the sound filled the whole stairwell. Unfortunately this flight of the chief clerk now also seemed to confuse Gregor's father, who up to that point had been relatively composed: instead of running after the chief clerk himself or at least not obstructing Gregor in *his* pursuit, with his right hand he seized the chief clerk's walking stick, which the latter had left behind on a chair along with his hat and overcoat; with his left hand he gathered up a big newspaper from the table and, stamping his feet, began to drive Gregor back into his room by brandishing the walking stick and the paper. No plea of Gregor's helped; in fact, no plea was understood; no matter how humbly he turned his head, his father only stamped his feet harder. On the other side of the room his mother had torn open a window despite the cool weather, and, leaning out, was pressing her face into her hands far beyond the window frame. Between the street and the stairwell a strong draught was created, the window curtains flew up, the newspapers on the table rustled and a few sheets blew across the floor. Implacably the father urged him back, uttering hisses like a savage. Gregor, however, had no practice in walking backwards, and, to tell the truth, it was very slow going for him. If Gregor had only been able to turn around, he would have been back in his room right away, but he was afraid of making his father impatient by such a time-consuming turn, and at every moment he was threatened by a fatal blow on the back or head from the stick in his father's hand. But finally Gregor had no other choice, because he observed with horror that, when walking backwards, he wasn't even able to keep in one direction; and so, with uninterrupted, anguished sidewise glances at his father, he began to turn around as quickly as he could, but nevertheless very slowly. Perhaps his father noticed his good will, because he didn't disturb him in this procedure but from time to time even conducted the rotary movement from a distance with the tip of his stick. If only his father had stopped that unbearable hissing! It made Gregor lose his head altogether. He was almost completely turned around when, constantly on the alert for that hissing, he made a mistake and turned himself back again a little. But when at last he had happily brought his head around to the opening in the doorway, it turned out that his body was too wide to get through without further difficulty. Naturally, in his present mood it didn't even remotely occur to his father to open the other leaf of the door in order to create an adequate passageway for Gregor. His idée fixe was merely that Gregor was to get into his room as quickly as possible. Nor would he ever have allowed the circumstantial preparations that were necessary for Gregor to hoist himself upright and perhaps get through the door in that way. Instead, as if there were no obstacle, he was now driving Gregor forward and making a lot of noise about it; what Gregor now heard behind him was no longer anything like the voice of merely one father; it was really no longer a joking matter, and Gregor squeezed into the doorway, no matter what the consequences. One side of his body lifted itself up; he was lying obliquely in the opening; one of his sides was completely abraded; ugly stains were left on the white door; now he was stuck tight and wouldn't have been able to stir from the spot; on one side his little legs were hanging up in the air and trembling, those on the other side were painfully crushed on the ground — then his father gave him a strong push from behind that was a truly liberating one, and, bleeding profusely, he sailed far into his room. Next, the door was slammed shut with the stick, then all was finally quiet.

II

IT WAS ONLY at twilight that Gregor awoke from his deep, swoonlike sleep. He would surely have awakened not much later even if there had been no disturbance, because he felt sufficiently rested and refreshed by sleep, but it seemed to him as if he had been aroused by a hasty footfall and a cautious locking of the door that led to the hallway. The light of the electric street lamps lay pallidly here and there on the ceiling and on the upper parts of the furniture, but down where Gregor was, it was dark. Slowly, still feeling his way clumsily with his antennae, which he was just now beginning to appreciate, he heaved himself over to the door to see what had happened there. His left side seemed to be one long scar, with an unpleasant tightness to it, and he actually had to limp on his two rows of legs. In addition, one leg had been severely damaged during the morning's events — it was a almost a miracle that only one had been damaged — and now dragged after him lifelessly.

It was only when he had reached the door that he noticed what had really lured him there; it was the aroma of something edible. For a basin stood there, filled with milk in which little slices of white bread were floating. He could almost have laughed for joy, because he was even hungrier than in the morning, and immediately he plunged his head into the milk almost over his eyes. But soon he pulled it out again in disappointment; it was not only that eating caused him difficulties because of his tender left side — and he could eat only when his whole body participated, puffing away — on top of that, he didn't at all like the milk, which was formerly his favorite beverage and which therefore had surely been placed there by his sister for that very reason; in fact, he turned away from the basin almost with repugnance and crept back to the center of the room.

In the parlor, as Gregor saw through the crack in the door, the gas was lit, but, whereas usually at that time of day his father was accustomed to read his afternoon paper to his mother, and sometimes his sister, in a loud voice, now there was not a sound to be heard. Maybe that practice of reading aloud, which his sister always told and wrote him about, had fallen out of use recently. But it was so quiet all around, too, even though the apartment was surely not empty. "What a quiet life the family leads," Gregor said to himself, and while he stared ahead into the darkness, he felt very proud of himself for having been able to provide his parents and sister with a life like that, in such a beautiful apartment. But what if now all the peace, all the prosperity, all the contentment were to come to a fearful end? In order not to give way to such thoughts, Gregor preferred to start moving, and he crawled back and forth in the room.

Once during the long evening one of the side doors, and once the other one, was opened a tiny crack and swiftly shut again; someone had probably needed to come in but was too disinclined to do so. Now Gregor came to a halt directly in front of the parlor door, determined to bring in the hesitant visitor in some way or another, or else at least find out who it was; but the door wasn't opened again and Gregor waited in vain. That morning, when the doors were locked, they had all wanted to come into his room; now, after he had himself opened one door and the others had obviously been opened during the day, no one came any longer, and, in addition, the keys were now on the outside.

It wasn't until late at night that the light in the parlor was turned off, and now it was easy to ascertain that his parents and sister had been up all that time, because, as could clearly be heard, all three now stole away on tiptoe. Surely no one would come into Gregor's room any more before morning, and so he had plenty of time in which to think without disturbance about how he should now reorganize his life. But the high, open room, in which he was compelled to lie flat on the floor, filled him with anguish, although he couldn't discover the reason for it, because, after all, it was the room he had occupied for five years — and, making a semiconscious turn, not without a slight feeling of shame, he dashed under the couch, where, even though his back was a little squeezed and he could no longer lift his head, he immediately felt quite comfortable, only regretting that his body was too wide to fit under the couch completely.

There he remained the whole night, which he spent partly in a half-slumber, from which he was startled awake time and again by hunger, and partly in worries and ill-defined hopes, all of which led to the conclusion that for the time being he had to stay calm and, by exercising patience and being as considerate as possible to his family, make bearable the unpleasantness that he was absolutely compelled to cause them in his present condition.

By the early morning, when the night had barely passed, Gregor had the opportunity to test the strength of his newly made resolutions, because his sister, almost fully dressed, opened the door from the hallway side and looked in uneasily. She didn't catch sight of him at once, but when she noticed him under the couch — God, he had to be somewhere, he couldn't have flown away — she received such a fright that, unable to control herself, she slammed the door again from outside. But, as if regretting her behavior, she immediately opened the door again and walked in on tiptoe as if she were visiting a seriously ill person or even a stranger. Gregor had moved his head out almost to the edge of the couch, and was observing her. Would she notice that he had left the milk standing, and by no means because he wasn't hungry, and would she bring some other food that suited him better? If she didn't do so of her own accord, he would rather starve to death than call it to her attention, even though in reality he had a tremendous urge to shoot out from under the couch, throw himself at his sister's feet and ask her for something good to eat. But his sister immediately noticed with surprise that the basin was still full, and that only a little milk had been spilled out of it all around; she picked it up at once, not with her bare hands, of course, but with a rag, and carried it out. Gregor was extremely curious to see what she would bring to replace it, and the most varied things came to mind. But he could never have guessed what his sister in her kindness actually did. In order to test his likings, she brought him a big selection, all spread out on an old newspaper. There were old, half-rotten vegetables; bones from their supper, coated with a white gravy that had solidified; a few raisins and almonds; a cheese that two days earlier Gregor would have considered inedible; a dry slice of bread, a slice of bread and butter, and a slice of salted bread and butter. In addition she set down the basin that had probably been designated permanently for Gregor; she had now poured water into it. And from a feeling of delicacy, since she knew Gregor wouldn't eat in her presence, she withdrew hastily and even turned the key in the lock so that Gregor would see he could make himself as comfortable as he wished. Gregor's little legs whirred as he now moved toward the food. Moreover, his wounds must have completely healed by this time; he felt no more hindrance. He was amazed at that, remembering how, more than a month earlier, he had cut his finger slightly with a knife and how that cut had still hurt him considerably even the day before yesterday. "Am I less sensitive now?" he thought, and was already greedily sucking on the cheese, which had attracted him immediately and imperatively more than any of the other foods. Quickly, one after the other, tears of contentment coming to his eyes, he devoured the cheese, the vegetables and the gravy; on the other hand, he didn't like the fresh food, he couldn't even endure its smell, and he went so far as to drag away to a little distance the things he wanted to eat. He was long finished with everything and was just lying lazily on the same spot when, as a sign that he should withdraw, his sister slowly turned the key. That startled him at once, even though he was almost drowsing by that time, and he hastened back under the couch. But it took enormous self-control to stay under the couch for even the brief time his sister was in the room, because the hearty meal had swelled his body to some extent, and he could hardly breathe in that cramped space. In between brief bouts of asphyxia, with slightly protruding eyes he watched his unsuspecting sister sweep together with a broom not only the leftovers of what he had eaten, but even the foods Gregor hadn't touched at all, as if those too were no longer usable; and he saw how she hastily dropped everything into a bucket, which she closed with a wooden cover, and then carried everything out. She had scarcely turned around when Gregor moved out from under the couch, stretched and let himself expand.

In this manner Gregor received his food every day, once in the morning, while his parents and the maid were still asleep, and the second time after everyone's midday meal, because then his parents took a short nap and the maid was sent away by his sister on some errand. Surely *they* didn't want Gregor to starve, either, but perhaps they couldn't have endured the experience of his eating habits except through hearsay; perhaps his sister also wanted to spare them one more sorrow, though possibly only a small one, because they were really suffering enough as it was.

Gregor couldn't find out what excuses had been used on that first morning to get the doctor and the locksmith out of the apartment again, because the others, even his sister, not understanding him, had no idea that *he* could understand *them*; and so, when his sister was in his room, he had to content himself with hearing her occasional sighs and invocations of the saints. Only later, when they had gotten used to it all to some degree — naturally, their ever getting used to it altogether was out of the question — Gregor sometimes seized on a remark that was meant to be friendly or could be so interpreted. "He really liked it today," she said when Gregor had stowed away his food heartily, whereas, when the opposite was the case, which gradually occurred more and more frequently, she used to say almost sadly: "This time he didn't touch anything again."

But even though Gregor couldn't learn any news directly, he overheard many things from the adjoining rooms, and whenever the sound of voices reached him, he would immediately run to the appropriate door and press his whole body against it. Especially in the early days there was no conversation that didn't deal with him in some way, if only in secret. At every mealtime for two days he could hear discussions about how they should now behave; but between meals, as well, they spoke on the same subject, because there were at least two family members at home at any given time, since no one apparently wanted to stay home alone and yet the apartment could in no case be deserted altogether. Besides, on the very first day the servant — it was not quite clear what or how much she knew of the incident — had asked Gregor's mother on her knees to discharge her at once, and when she said good-bye fifteen minutes later, she thanked them tearfully for letting her go, as if that were the greatest benefit they could confer upon her, and, without being asked to do so, swore a fearsome oath that she would never reveal the slightest thing to anyone.

Now Gregor's sister had to join their mother in doing the cooking; of course that didn't entail much effort because they ate practically nothing. Time and again Gregor heard them fruitlessly urge one another to eat, receiving no other answer than "Thanks, I've had enough" or the like. Maybe they didn't drink anything, either. Often his sister asked their father whether he wanted any beer, and offered lovingly to fetch it herself; then, as the father remained silent, she said, to overcome any reservations he might have, that she could also send the janitor's wife for it, but finally the father would utter a decided "No" and the matter was discussed no further.

Even in the course of the first day the father already laid their entire financial situation and prospects before both the mother and the sister. From time to time he got up from the table and took some document or some memorandum book out of his small Wertheim* safe, which he had held onto even after the collapse of his business five years earlier. He could be heard opening the complicated lock and closing it again after

* [An Austrian brand of safe widely used by businessmen at the time. — TRANSLATOR.]

removing what he had been looking for. In part, these declarations by his father were the first heartening things Gregor had heard since his captivity. He had believed that his father had nothing at all left from that business — at least, his father had never told him anything to the contrary — and naturally Gregor hadn't asked him about it. Gregor's concern at the time had been to do everything in his power to make his family forget as quickly as possible the commercial disaster that had reduced them all to complete hopelessness. And so, at that time he had begun to work with extreme enthusiasm and almost overnight had changed from a junior clerk into a traveling salesman; as such, he naturally had many more possibilities of earning money, and his successful efforts were immediately transformed into cash in the form of commissions, cash that could be plunked down on the table at home before the eyes of his amazed and delighted family. Those had been good times and had never been repeated later, at least not so gloriously, even though Gregor subsequently earned so much money that he was enabled to shoulder the expenses of the entire family, and did so. They had grown used to it, the family as well as Gregor; they accepted the money gratefully, he handed it over gladly, but no particularly warm feelings were generated any longer. Only his sister had still remained close to Gregor all the same, and it was his secret plan — because, unlike Gregor, she dearly loved music and could play the violin soulfully — to send her to the conservatory the following year, regardless of the great expenses which that had to entail, and which would have to be made up for in some other way. Often during Gregor's brief sojourns in the city the conservatory was referred to in his conversations with his sister, but always merely as a lovely dream, which couldn't possibly come true, and their parents disliked hearing even those innocent references; but Gregor was planning it most resolutely and intended to make a formal announcement on Christmas Eve.

Thoughts like those, completely pointless in his present state, occupied his mind while he stood upright there, pasting his legs to the door and listening. Sometimes, out of total weariness, he could no longer listen and let his head knock carelessly against the door, but immediately held it firm again, because even the slight noise he had caused by doing so had been heard in the next room and had made everyone fall silent. "How he keeps carrying on!" his father would say after a pause, obviously looking toward the door, and only then was the interrupted conversation gradually resumed.

Because his father used to repeat himself frequently in his explanations — partly because he hadn't concerned himself with these things for some time, partly also because the mother didn't understand it all the first time — Gregor had full opportunity to ascertain that, despite all their misfortune, a sum of money, of course very small, was still left over from the old days and had grown somewhat in the interim, since the interest had never been touched. And, besides that, the money Gregor had brought home every month — he had kept only a few *gulden* for himself — had not been completely used up and amounted to a small capital. Gregor, behind his door, nodded vigorously, delighted by this unexpected foresight and thrift. To tell the truth, with that surplus money he could have further reduced his father's debt to his boss, and the day when he could get rid of that job would have been much closer, but now it was without a doubt better the way his father had arranged it.

Now, this money was by no means sufficient for the family even to think of living off the interest; it might suffice to maintain the family for one or, at the most, two years, no more than that. It was thus merely a sum that should really not be drawn upon, but only kept in reserve for an emergency; money to live on had to be earned. Now, the father was a healthy man, to be sure, but old; he hadn't done any work for five years and in any case couldn't be expected to overexert himself; in those five years, which represented his first free time in a laborious though unsuccessful life, he had put on a lot of fat and had thus become pretty slow-moving. And was Gregor's old mother perhaps supposed to earn money now, a victim of asthma, for whom an excursion across the apartment was already cause for strain, and who spent every other day on the sofa by the open window gasping for breath? And was his sister supposed to earn money, at seventeen still a child whom one could hardly begrudge the way she had always lived up to now: dressing nicely, sleeping late, helping out in the house, enjoying a few modest amusements and, most of all, playing the violin? Whenever the conversation led to this necessity of earning money, Gregor would always first let go of the door and then throw himself onto the cool leather sofa located next to the door, because he was hot all over with shame and sorrow.

Often he would lie there all through the long nights, not sleeping for a minute but only scratching on the leather for hours on end. At other times he didn't spare the exertion of shoving a chair over to the window; he would then crawl up the ledge and, supporting himself against the chair, lean against the window, obviously only through some sort of recollection of the liberating feeling he always used to experience when looking out the window. Because, in reality, with each passing day his view of things at only a slight distance was becoming increasingly blurry; the hospital opposite, the all-too-frequent sight of which he used to curse, he now could no longer see at all, and if he hadn't been perfectly well aware that he lived on the tranquil but thoroughly urban Charlottenstrasse, he might have thought that what he saw from his window was a featureless solitude, in which the gray sky and the gray earth blended inseparably. His attentive sister had only needed to notice twice that the chair was standing by the window, and now, each time she had finished cleaning up the room, she shoved the chair right back to the window, and from that time on even left the inner casement open.

If Gregor had only been able to speak with his sister and thank her for all she had to do for him, he would have endured her services more easily; but, as it was, they made him suffer. Of course, his sister tried to soften the painfulness of the situation as much as possible, and as more and more time went by, she was naturally more successful at it, but with time Gregor, too, made a much keener analysis of everything. Her very entrance was terrible for him. The moment she walked in, without taking the time to close the door, even though she was otherwise most careful to spare everyone the sight of Gregor's room, she ran straight to the window and tore it open hastily, as if she were almost suffocating, and then remained a while at the window breathing deeply, no matter how cold it was. She frightened Gregor twice a day with that running and noise; during the whole time, he trembled under the couch, even though he knew perfectly well that she would surely have spared him that gladly if she had been at all capable of staying in a room containing Gregor with the window closed.

Once — probably a month had already elapsed since Gregor's transformation, and his sister should no longer have had any particular reason to be surprised at Gregor's appearance — she came a little earlier than usual and encountered Gregor while he was still looking out the window, motionless and posed there like some hideous scarecrow. It wouldn't have surprised Gregor if she hadn't stepped in, since by his location he was preventing her from opening the window at once; but not only did she not step in, she even jumped back and closed the door; a stranger might even have thought that Gregor had been lying in wait for her, intending to bite her. Naturally, Gregor immediately hid under the couch, but he had to wait until noon before his sister returned, and she seemed much more restless than usual. From this he realized that the sight of him was still unbearable for her and would surely remain unbearable for her in the future, and that she probably had to exercise terrific self-control not to run away at the sight of even the small portion of his body that protruded below the couch. To spare her even that sight, one day — he needed four hours for this task — he carried the bedsheet on his back over to the couch and draped it in such a way that he was now completely covered and his sister couldn't see him even when she bent down. If that sheet, in her opinion, hadn't been necessary, she could have removed it, because it was clear enough that it was no pleasure for Gregor to close himself off so completely; but she left the sheet where it was, and Gregor believed he caught a grateful look when he once cautiously raised the sheet a little with his head to see how his sister reacted to the new arrangement.

In the first two weeks his parents couldn't muster the courage to come into his room, and he often heard them expressing complete satisfaction with the work his sister was now doing, whereas up to that time they had frequently been vexed with his sister because she had seemed a rather good-for-nothing girl to them. But often now, both of them, the father and the mother, waited in front of Gregor's room while his sister was cleaning up in there, and the moment she came out she had to report in detail on how the room looked, what Gregor had eaten, how he had behaved this time, and whether a slight improvement could perhaps be noticed. As it was, the mother wanted to visit Gregor relatively early on, but at first the father and the sister held her back with sensible reasons, which Gregor listened to most attentively, and which he fully concurred with. Later, however, she had to be restrained forcefully, and when she then called: "Let me in to Gregor; after all, he's my poor son! Don't you understand I must go to him?," Gregor thought it might be a good thing after all if his mother came in, not every day of course, but perhaps once a week; after all, she understood everything much better than his sister, who, despite all her spunk, was still only a child and, in the final analysis, had perhaps undertaken such a difficult task only out of child-ish thoughtlessness.

Gregor's wish to see his mother was soon fulfilled. During the day Gregor didn't want to show himself at the window, if only out of consideration for his parents, but he also couldn't crawl very much on the few square yards of the floor; even at night he found it difficult to lie still. Soon he no longer derived the slightest pleasure from eating, either, and so for amusement he acquired the habit of crawling in all directions across the walls and ceiling. He especially enjoyed hanging up on the ceiling; it was quite different from lying on the floor; one could breathe more easily; a mild vibration passed through his body; and in the almost happy forgetfulness that Gregor experienced up there, it sometimes happened that to his own surprise he let go and crashed onto the floor. But now he naturally had much greater control over his body than before and even such a great fall did him no harm. Now, his sister immediately noticed this new diversion that Gregor had discov-ered for himself — even when crawling he left behind traces of his sticky substance here and there — and then she got the notion of enabling

Gregor to crawl around as freely as possible, by removing the furniture that prevented this, especially the wardrobe and the desk. But she was unable to do this on her own; she didn't dare ask her father to help; the servant surely wouldn't have helped her, because even though this girl of about sixteen was sticking it out bravely since the previous cook had been discharged, she had nevertheless requested permission to keep the kitchen locked at all times and to open it only when specially called; thus the sister had no other choice than to fetch her mother while the father was away one day. And the mother approached with exclamations of excitement and joy, but fell silent at the door to Gregor's room. Naturally, the sister looked in first to see if everything in the room was in order; only then did she allow the mother to enter. Gregor had in extreme haste pulled the sheet even lower down, making more folds in it; the whole thing really looked like a sheet that had been thrown over the couch merely by chance. Also, this time Gregor refrained from peering out from under the sheet; he gave up the opportunity of seeing his mother this first time, in his happiness that she had finally come. "Come on, you can't see him," said the sister, and obviously she was leading the mother by the hand. Gregor now heard how the two weak women moved the old wardrobe, heavy as it was, from its place, and how the sister constantly undertook the greater part of the work, paying no heed to the warnings of the mother, who feared she would overexert herself. It took a very long time. After about a quarter-hour's work the mother said it would be better to leave the wardrobe where it was, because, for one thing, it was too heavy, they wouldn't get through before the father arrived, and, with the wardrobe in the middle of the room, they would leave Gregor no open path; and, secondly, it was not at all certain that Gregor would be pleased by the removal of the furniture. She thought the opposite was the case; the sight of the bare wall actually made her heart ache; and why shouldn't Gregor, too, feel the same way, since after all he was long accustomed to the furniture in his room and would thus feel isolated in the empty room? "And, besides, doesn't it seem," the mother concluded very quietly — throughout her speech she had been almost whispering, as if she wanted to keep Gregor, whose exact where-abouts she didn't know, from hearing even the sound of her voice (she was convinced he didn't understand the words) — "and doesn't it seem as if, by removing the furniture, we were showing that we have given up all hope for an improvement and were inconsiderately leaving him to his own resources? I think it would be best if we tried to keep the room in exactly the same condition as before, so that when Gregor comes back to us again, he'll find everything unchanged and it will be easier for him to forget what happened in between."

On hearing these words of his mother's, Gregor realized that the lack of all direct human communication, together with the monotonous life in the midst of the family, must have confused his mind in the course of these two months, because he couldn't explain to himself otherwise how he could seriously have wished for his room to be emptied out. Did he really want to have the warm room, comfortably furnished with heirloom pieces, transformed into a cave, in which he would, of course, be able to crawl about freely in all directions, but at the cost of simultaneously forgetting his human past, quickly and totally? Even now he was close to forgetting it, and only his mother's voice, which he hadn't heard for some time, had awakened him to the fact. Nothing must be removed, everything must stay; he couldn't do without the beneficent effects of the furniture on his well-being; and if the furniture prevented him from going on with that mindless crawling around, that was no disadvantage, but a great asset.

Unfortunately, however, his sister was of a different opinion; not without some justification, true, she had grown accustomed to play herself up to her parents as a special expert whenever matters affecting Gregor were discussed; and so now, too, the mother's advice was cause enough for the sister to insist on the removal of not only the wardrobe and the desk, which were all she had thought of at first, but all the furniture, except for the indispensable couch. Naturally, it was not only childish defiance and the self-confidence she had recently acquired so unexpectedly and with such great efforts, that determined her to make this demand; she had also made the real observation that Gregor needed a lot of space to crawl in, while on the other hand he didn't use the furniture in the least, from all one could see. But perhaps a further element was the romantic spirit of girls of her age, which seeks for satisfaction on every occasion, and by which Grete now let herself be tempted to make Gregor's situation even more frightful, so that she could do even more for him than hitherto — because nobody except Grete would ever dare to enter a space in which Gregor on his own dominated the bare walls.

And so she wouldn't let herself be dissuaded by her mother, who seemed unsure of herself, as well, in that room, out of sheer nervousness, and who soon fell silent, helping the sister move out the wardrobe with all her might. Now, in an emergency Gregor could still do without the wardrobe, but the desk — that had to stay. And no sooner had the women left the room with the wardrobe, which they were pushing while emitting groans, than Gregor thrust out his head from under the couch to see how he could intervene cautiously and with the greatest possible consideration for them. But, as bad luck would have it, it was his mother who came back first, while Grete in the adjoining room had her arms around the wardrobe and was swinging it back and forth unaided, naturally without being able to move it from the spot. But the mother wasn't used to the sight of Gregor, which might make her sick, so in a panic Gregor hastened backwards up to the other end of the couch but could no longer prevent the sheet from stirring a little in front. That was enough to attract his mother's attention. She stopped in her tracks, stood still a moment and then went back to Grete.

Although Gregor told himself over and over that nothing unusual was going on, just a few pieces of furniture being moved around, he soon had to admit to himself that this walking to and fro by the women, their brief calls to each other and the scraping of the furniture on the floor affected him like a tremendous uproar, sustained on all sides; and, no matter how tightly he pulled in his head and legs and pressed his body all the way to the floor, he was irresistibly compelled to tell himself that he wouldn't be able to endure all of this very long. They were emptying out his room, taking away from him everything he was fond of; they had already carried out the wardrobe, which contained his fretsaw and other tools; now they were prying loose the desk, which had long been firmly entrenched in the floor, and at which he had done his homework when he was in business college, in secondary school and even back in primary school. At this point, he really had no more time for testing the good intentions of the two women, whose existence he had almost forgotten, anyway, because in their state of exhaustion they were now working in silence, and only their heavy footfalls could be heard.

And so he broke out — at the moment, the women were leaning on the desk in the adjoining room, to catch their breath a little — he changed direction four times, not really knowing what he should rescue first; and then he saw hanging conspicuously on the now otherwise bare wall the picture of the lady dressed in nothing but furs. He crawled up to it in haste and pressed against the glass, which held him fast and felt good on his hot belly. That picture, at least, which Gregor was now completely covering, surely no one would now take away. He twisted his head around toward the door of the parlor in order to observe the women when they returned.

They hadn't allowed themselves much time to rest, and were now coming back; Grete had put her arm around her mother and was almost carrying her. "Well, what should we take now?" said Grete and looked around. Then her eyes met those of Gregor on the wall. It was probably only because her mother was there that she kept her composure; she lowered her face to her mother to keep her from looking around, and said, although tremblingly and without thinking: "Come, shouldn't we rather go back into the parlor for another minute?" Grete's intention was clear to Gregor; she wanted to lead her mother to safety and then chase him down off the wall. Well, just let her try! He sat there on his picture and wouldn't relinquish it. He would sooner jump onto Grete's face.

But Grete's words had been just what it took to upset her mother, who stepped to one side, caught sight of the gigantic brown spot on the flowered wallpaper, and, before she was actually aware that what she saw there was Gregor, called in a hoarse shout: "Oh, God, oh, God!" She then fell across the couch with outspread arms, as if giving up everything, and lay there perfectly still. "Just wait, Gregor!" called the sister with raised fist and piercing glances. Those were the first words she had addressed to him directly since the transformation. She ran into the adjoining room to fetch some medicine to revive her mother from her faint; Gregor wanted to help, too — there was still time to rescue the picture — but he was stuck tight to the glass and had to tear himself loose by force. Then he, too, ran into the adjoining room, as if he could give his sister some advice, as in the past; but he was forced to stand behind her idly. While she was rummaging among various little bottles, she got a fright when she turned around; a bottle fell on the floor and broke; a splinter wounded Gregor in the face, and some kind of corrosive medicine poured over him. Now, without waiting there any longer, Grete picked up as many bottles as she could hold and ran in to her mother with them, slamming the door shut with her foot. Gregor was now cut off from his mother, who was perhaps close to death, all on his account. He didn't dare open the door for fear of driving away his sister, who had to remain with their mother. Now there was nothing for him to do but wait; and oppressed by self-reproaches and worry, he began to crawl; he crawled all over everything, walls, furniture and ceiling, and finally, in his desperation, when the whole room was starting to spin around him, he fell onto the middle of the big table.

A brief while passed, Gregor lay there limply, it was quiet all around; maybe that was a good sign. Then the bell rang. Naturally, the servant was locked in her kitchen, and so Grete had to go open up. Her father had arrived. "What's happened?" were his first words; Grete's appearance had probably revealed everything to him. Grete answered in a muffled voice, probably pressing her face against her father's chest: "Mother fainted, but she's feeling better now. Gregor has broken loose." "I expected it," said the father, "I always told you so, but you women won't listen." It was clear to Gregor that his father had put a bad interpretation on Grete's excessively brief communication and assumed that Gregor had been guilty of some act of violence. Therefore Gregor now had to try to pacify his father, because he had neither the time nor the means to enlighten him. And so he sped away to the door of his room and pressed himself against it, so that when his father came in from the hallway he could immediately see that Gregor fully intended to return to his room at once, and that it was unnecessary to chase him back; instead, all they needed to do was to open the door, and he would disappear right away.

But his father was in no mood to observe such niceties; as soon as he walked in, he yelled "Ah!" in a tone that suggested he was both furious and happy at the same time. Gregor drew his head back from the door and lifted it toward his father. He hadn't really pictured his father the way he now stood there; recently, to be sure, he had been so occupied by the new sensation of crawling around that he had neglected to pay attention to events in the rest of the apartment, as he had done earlier; and he should really have been prepared to encounter altered circumstances. And yet, and yet, was this still his father? The same man who would lie wearily, buried in his bed, when Gregor used to "move out smartly" on a business trip; who had received him wearing a bathrobe and sitting in an armchair when he returned home in the evening; who hadn't been fully capable of standing up, and had merely raised his arms as a sign of joy; who, during their rare family strolls on a few Sundays of the year and on the major holidays, would walk between Gregor and his mother, who walked slowly even on their own, but would always be a little slower yet, bundled up in his old coat and working his way forward with his crook-handled stick always placed cautiously before him; who, when he wanted to say something, almost always came to a halt and gathered the rest of the group around him? Now, however, he was perfectly erect, dressed in a tight blue uniform with gold buttons, like those worn by messengers in banking houses. Above the high, stiff collar of the jacket his pronounced double chin unfurled; below his bushy eyebrows the gaze of his dark eyes shone brightly and observantly; his usually tousled white hair was combed down flat and gleaming, with a painfully exact part. He threw his hat, which was adorned by a gold monogram, probably that of some bank, in an arc across the whole room onto the couch; and, pushing back the tails of his long uniform jacket, his hands in his trousers pockets, he walked toward Gregor with a morose expression. He most likely had no idea himself of what he intended to do; nevertheless, he raised his feet unusually high, and Gregor was amazed at the gigantic size of his boot soles. But he didn't dwell on that, for he had known ever since the first day of his new life that his father considered nothing but the greatest severity appropriate where he was concerned. And so he ran in front of his father, came to a halt when his father stood still and immediately sprinted forward if his father made any kind of move. In that way they circled the room several times, without anything decisive occurring; in fact, because of the slow tempo the whole thing didn't have the appearance of a pursuit. For that reason, as well, Gregor stayed on the floor for the time being, especially because he was afraid that his father might look upon a scurry onto the walls or ceiling as being particularly malicious. And yet Gregor had to tell himself that even the present activity would soon be too much for him, because for every step his father took he had to execute a huge number of movements. Shortness of breath was already becoming noticeable, and even in his earlier days his lungs hadn't been the most reliable. As he was now staggering along, in order to gather all his strength for running, and could barely keep his eyes open — unable, in his dazed condition, to think of any other refuge than running, and almost forgetting that the walls were open to him (although in this room they were obstructed by painstakingly carved furniture full of prongs and points) — something that had been lightly tossed flew right by him and rolled in front of him on the floor. It was an apple; another flew at him immediately afterward; Gregor stood still in fright; to continue running was pointless, because his father had decided to bombard him. He had filled his pockets from the fruit bowl on the sideboard and now, without aiming carefully for the moment, was throwing one apple after another. A weakly thrown apple grazed Gregor's back, but rolled off harmlessly. One that flew right after it actually penetrated Gregor's back; Gregor wanted to drag himself onward, as if the surprising and unbelievable pain might pass if he changed location; but he felt pinned down and he surrendered, all his senses fully bewildered. It was only with his last glance that he still saw the door of his room being torn open; he saw his mother dash out ahead of his screaming sister (the mother was in her shift, because the sister had undressed her to make it easier for her to breathe when she had fainted); he then saw the mother run over to the father, her untied petticoats slipping to the floor one after the other as she went. Tripping over the petticoats, she rushed upon the father and, embracing him, in absolute union with him — at this point all went dark for Gregor — with her hands behind the father's head, she begged him to spare Gregor's life.

III

GREGOR'S SEVERE INJURY, from which he suffered for more than a month — since no one dared to remove the apple, it remained in his flesh as a visible reminder — seemed to have made even his father recall that, despite his present sad and disgusting shape, Gregor was a member of the family who shouldn't be treated as an enemy, but in whose case family obligations demanded that one swallow one's repulsion and be patient, only patient.

And even if Gregor's wound had probably impaired his mobility for good, and he now, like an old invalid, needed long, long minutes to cross his room — crawling up high was out of the question — he received in exchange for this worsening of his condition something he considered a perfectly adequate replacement: as every evening approached, the parlor door, which he would begin to watch carefully an hour or two ahead of time, was opened so that, lying in the dark, invisible from the parlor, he could see the whole family at the brightly lit table and listen to their conversation, to some extent with everyone's permission, and thus quite otherwise than before.

Of course, these were no longer the lively discussions of the old days, to which Gregor's thoughts had always turned with some yearning in his tiny hotel rooms, when he had had to throw himself wearily into the damp bedclothes. Generally the talks were very quiet. Right after supper the father fell asleep in his chair; the mother and sister admonished each other to be quiet; the mother, leaning far forward under the light, sewed fine linen for a clothing store; the sister, who had taken work as a salesgirl, was learning stenography and French at night so that she might possibly get a better job some day. At times the father woke up and, as if he didn't even know he'd been sleeping, he said to the mother: "How long you've been sewing again today!" and went right back to sleep, while mother and sister smiled at each other wearily.

With a sort of obstinacy the father refused to take off his messenger's uniform even at home; and while his bathrobe hung unused on the hook, the father drowsed in his chair fully dressed, as if he were always ready to do his work and were awaiting his superior's orders even here. Consequently, despite all the mother and sister's care, the uniform, which hadn't been brand new at the outset, became less and less clean; and often for entire evenings Gregor would look at this garment, stained all over, but with constantly polished and gleaming gold buttons, in which the old man slept in great discomfort and yet peacefully.

The moment the clock struck ten, the mother tried to wake the father by addressing him softly and then tried to convince him to go to bed, because here he couldn't get any proper sleep, which the father needed very badly, since he had to begin work at six. But with the obstinacy that had taken hold of him since he had become a messenger, he constantly insisted on remaining longer at the table, although he regularly fell asleep, and then, on top of that, could only be persuaded with the greatest difficulty to give up his chair for his bed. In this situation mother and sister might urge him over and over with little reminders, for periods of fifteen minutes at a time he would shake his head slowly, keep his eyes closed and refuse to stand up. The mother tugged at his sleeve and said sweet things in his ear, the sister would leave her task to help the mother, but this had no effect on the father. He merely sank more deeply into his chair. Only when the women seized him under his arms would he open his eyes, look now at the mother and now at the sister, and say: "This is living! This is the repose of my old age!" And, supported by the two women, he would get up, slowly and fussily, as if he were his own greatest burden, and would allow himself to be led to the door by the women; there he would wave them away and proceed on his own, while the mother hastily flung down her sewing things and the sister her pen in order to run after the father and continue to be of service to him.

In this overworked and overtired family, who had time to be concerned about Gregor beyond what was absolutely necessary? There were constant retrenchments in their way of living; they finally had to let the servant go; a gigantic, bony cleaning woman with white hair fluttering around her head now came in the morning and evening to do the heaviest chores; everything else was attended to by the mother, who also had all that sewing to do. It even came to pass that various pieces of family jewelry, which the mother and sister had formerly worn at parties and on great occasions, were sold, as Gregor learned in the evening from the family's discussion of the prices they had received. But the greatest complaint always was that they couldn't leave this apartment, which was far too big for their present means, since no one could figure out how to move Gregor. But Gregor realized that it was not only the concern for him that prevented a move, because after all he could easily have been shipped in a suitable crate with a few air holes; what principally kept the family from changing apartments was rather the complete hopelessness of the situation and the thought that they had been afflicted with a misfortune unlike any other in their entire circle of relatives and acquaintances. They were performing to the hilt all that the world demands of poor people: the father carried in breakfast for the junior bank clerks, the mother sacrificed herself for the linen of strangers, the sister ran back and forth behind her counter at the customers' command, but by this time the family's strength was taxed to the limit. And the sore on his back began to hurt Gregor all over again when, after putting his father to bed, his mother and sister came back, let their work rest, moved close together and sat cheek to cheek; when the mother, pointing to Gregor's room, now said, "Close the door there, Grete," and Gregor was again in the dark, while in the next room the women wept together or just stared at the table with dry eyes.

Gregor spent the nights and days almost completely without sleep. Sometimes he thought that, the next time the door opened, he would once again take charge of the family's problems just as he used to; in his thoughts there reappeared, after a long interval, his boss and the chief clerk, the clerks and the apprentices, the office messenger who was so dense, two or three friends from other firms, a chambermaid in a provincial hotel (a charming, fleeting recollection), a cashier in a hat shop whom he had courted seriously but too slowly—they all appeared, mingling with strangers or people he'd forgotten, but instead of helping him and his family, they were all inaccessible, and he was glad when they disappeared. But at other times he was no longer at all in the mood to worry about his family; he was filled with nothing but rage over how badly he was looked after; and even though he couldn't imagine anything he might have had an appetite for, he laid plans for getting into the pantry so he could take what was still his by rights, even if he wasn't hungry. No longer reflecting about what might give Gregor some special pleasure, his sister now hastily shoved any old food into Gregor's room with her foot before running off to work in the morning and at noon; in the evening, not caring whether the food had perhaps been just merely tasted or— most frequently—left completely untouched, she would sweep it out with a swing of the broom. The cleaning of the room, which she now always took care of in the evening, was done at breakneck speed. Long trails of dirt lined the walls, here and there lay heaps of dust and filth. At first, when his sister arrived, Gregor would station himself at particularly glaring corners of that sort, thereby intending to reproach her to some degree. But he could have remained there for weeks on end without seeing any improvement in his sister; she saw the dirt just as well as he did, but she had simply made up her mind to leave it there. At the same time, with a touchiness that was quite new to her, and which had come over the whole family, she took care that the cleaning of Gregor's room should be reserved exclusively for her. On one occasion the mother had undertaken a thorough cleaning of Gregor's room, which she had only managed to do by using several buckets of water—the excessive dampness harmed Gregor, too, and he lay stretched out on the couch, embittered and motionless—but the mother didn't escape the penalty: the moment the sister noticed the change in Gregor's room in the evening, she ran into the parlor, highly insulted, and, despite the mother's imploringly uplifted hands, she broke into a crying jag that the parents—the father had naturally been frightened out of his chair—at first watched in amazement and helplessness until they themselves began to stir. To his right, the father reproached the mother for not leaving the cleaning of Gregor's room to the sister; to his left, on the other hand, he yelled at the sister, saying she would never again be permitted to clean Gregor's room, while the mother tried to drag the father, who was beside himself with agitation, into the bedroom; the sister, shaken with sobs, belabored the table with her little fists; and Gregor hissed loudly with rage because it didn't occur to anyone to close the door and spare him that sight and that commotion.

But even if the sister, worn out by her job, had grown tired of caring for Gregor as before, still the mother would not have been compelled to take over for her, and Gregor wouldn't have needed to be neglected. Because the cleaning woman was now there. This elderly widow, who, thanks to her powerful frame, had probably endured the worst during her long life, had no real horror of Gregor. Without being in the least curious, she had once accidentally opened the door to Gregor's room; at the sight of Gregor, who, taken by surprise, began to run back and forth although no one was chasing him, she had stood still in amazement, her hands folded over her stomach. Since then she never failed to open the door a little for just a moment in the morning and evening and to look in at Gregor. At the beginning she even called him over with words she probably thought were friendly, such as "Come on over here, old dung beetle" or "Just look at the old dung beetle!" Gregor never responded to such calls, but remained motionless where he stood, as if the door had never been opened. But if, instead of letting this cleaning woman disturb him needlessly as the fancy took her, they had only given her orders to clean his room every day! Once, early in the morning — a heavy rain, perhaps already foretokening the coming spring, was beating on the window panes — when the cleaning woman began with her series of expressions again, Gregor was so infuriated that he turned in her direction as if to attack, but slowly and feebly. The cleaning woman, however, instead of being frightened, merely lifted high in the air a chair that was near the door, and, as she stood there with her mouth wide open, she clearly intended not to close her mouth again until the chair in her hand crashed down on Gregor's back. "So you're not advancing?" she asked as Gregor turned around again, and placed the chair back calmly in the corner.

By this time Gregor was hardly eating. Only when he accidentally passed by the spread-out food would he take a bit in his mouth playfully, hold it there for hours and then generally spit it out again. At first he thought it was his dejection over the state of his room that kept him from eating, but he was soon more reconciled to the changes in his room than to anything else. They had grown accustomed to put in his room things there was no space for elsewhere, and there were now a lot of such things, because they had rented one room in the apartment to three lodgers. These serious gentlemen — all three had full beards, as Gregor once ascertained through a crack in the door — were sticklers for strict housekeeping, not only in their room, but also, since they were after all paying rent there, all over the apartment, and especially in the kitchen. They wouldn't stand for useless, not to mention dirty, odds and ends. Furthermore, they had for the most part brought along their own furnishings. Therefore many items had become superfluous that couldn't be sold but no one wanted to throw out. All of these were moved into Gregor's room. And so were the ash box and the garbage box from the kitchen. Whatever was unusable at the moment, the cleaning woman, who was always in a hurry, simply flung into Gregor's room; fortunately, Gregor generally saw only the object in question and the hand that held it. Perhaps the cleaning woman intended to retrieve the things when she had the time and opportunity, or to throw them all out at the same time, but in reality they remained wherever they had landed at the first toss, unless Gregor twisted through the rubbish and set it in motion, at first out of necessity, because no other space was open to crawl through, but later with increasing delight, although after such excursions, tired to death and dejected, he would again remain motionless for hours.

Since the lodgers sometimes also took their evening meal at home in the common parlor, the parlor door was closed on many evenings, but Gregor readily made do without the opening of the door, for on many earlier evenings when it was open he hadn't taken advantage of it, but instead, without the family noticing, had lain in the darkest corner of his room. But on one occasion the cleaning woman had left the door to the parlor a little open; and it remained open like that even when the lodgers entered in the evening and the light was turned on. They sat at the head of the table, where in earlier days the father, the mother and Gregor had sat; they unfolded their napkins and picked up their knives and forks. Immediately the mother appeared in the doorway with a platter of meat, and right behind her the sister with a plate piled high with potatoes. The food was steaming copiously. The lodgers bent over the plates that were placed in front of them as if wishing to examine them before eating, and, in fact, the one sitting in the middle, whom the others seemed to look up to as an authority, cut a piece of meat on the plate, obviously to ascertain whether it was tender enough and didn't perhaps need to be sent back to the kitchen. He was satisfied, and the mother and sister, who had watched in suspense, breathed easily and began to smile.

The family themselves ate in the kitchen. Nevertheless, before the father went into the kitchen, he entered the parlor and, with a single protracted bow, walked around the table, cap in hand. The lodgers all stood up and murmured something into their beards. Then, when they were alone, they ate with almost no conversation. It seemed odd to Gregor that, among all the multifarious noises of eating, their chewing teeth stood out again and again, as if to indicate to Gregor that teeth were indispensable for eating and that even with the finest toothless jaws nothing could be accomplished. "I do have an appetite," said Gregor uneasily to himself, "but not for those things. How these lodgers pack it away, and I'm perishing!"

On that very evening — Gregor had no recollection of having heard the violin during that whole time — it was audible from the kitchen. The lodgers had already finished their supper, the one in the middle had pulled out a newspaper, handing one sheet apiece to the two others, and now they were leaning back, reading and smoking. When the violin began to play, they noticed it, stood up and walked on tiptoe to the hallway door, remaining there in a tight group. They must have been heard in the kitchen, because the father called: "Does the playing perhaps bother you? We can stop it at once." "On the contrary," said the gentleman in the middle, "wouldn't the young lady like to come in here with us and play in this room, which is much more comfortable and cozy?" "Of course," called the father, as if *he* were the violinist. The gentlemen stepped back into the room and waited. Soon the father came with the music stand, the mother with the sheet music and the sister with the violin. The sister calmly put everything in readiness for playing; the parents, who had never rented out rooms before and therefore overdid the courtesy due to lodgers, didn't dare to sit on their own chairs; the father leaned on the door, his right hand placed between two buttons of his closed uniform jacket; but the mother was offered a chair by one of the gentlemen and, since she left the chair where the man happened to have placed it, she sat off to one side in a corner.

The sister began to play; the father and mother, each on his side, watched the motions of her hands closely. Gregor, attracted by the playing, had ventured out a little further and already had his head in the parlor. He was scarcely surprised that recently he was so little concerned about the feelings of the others; previously this considerateness had been his pride. As it was, right now he might have had even more cause to hide, because as a result of the dust that had settled all over in his room and blew around at the slightest movement, he was also completely covered with dust; he was dragging threads, hairs and crumbs of food around with him on his back and sides; his indifference to everything was much too great for him to turn over on his back and scour himself on the carpet, as he used to do several times a day. But despite being in this state, he had no qualms about moving a little bit forward on the immaculate floor of the parlor.

To be sure, no one was paying attention to him. The family was completely engrossed in the violin performance; on the other hand, the lodgers, who, hands in trousers pockets, had first of all moved their chairs much too close behind the sister's music stand, so that they could all have looked at the sheet music, which assuredly had to disturb the sister, soon withdrew, with semiaudible remarks and lowered heads, to the window, where they stayed put, watched by the father with concern. It was now abundantly evident that they were disappointed in their assumption that they were going to hear some pretty or entertaining violin music; they were clearly tired of the whole performance and were permitting their peace and quiet to be disturbed merely out of courtesy. It was especially the way they all blew their cigar smoke up into the air through their noses and mouths that indicated a terrific strain on their nerves. And yet the sister was playing beautifully. Her face was inclined to one side, her eyes followed the lines of music searchingly and sorrowfully. Gregor crawled a little bit further forward, keeping his head close to the floor in hopes of making eye contact with her. Was he an animal if music stirred him that way? He felt as if he were being shown the way to the unknown nourishment he longed for. He was resolved to push his way right up to his sister and tug at her skirt, as an indication to her to come into his room with her violin, because nobody here was repaying her for her playing the way he would repay her. He intended never to let her out of his room again, at least not as long as he lived; his horrifying shape was to be beneficial to him for the first time; he would be on guard at all the doors to his room at once, and spit at his assailants like a cat; but his sister would remain with him not under compulsion but voluntarily; she was to sit next to him on the couch and incline her ear toward him, and he would then confide to her that he had had the firm intention of sending her to the conservatory, and that, if the misfortune hadn't intervened, he would have told everyone so last Christmas — Christmas *was* over by now, wasn't it? — without listening to any objections. After this declaration his sister would burst into tears of deep emotion, and Gregor would raise himself to the level of her shoulder and kiss her neck, which, since she had begun her job, she had left bare, without any ribbon or collar.

"Mr. Samsa!" the gentleman in the middle called to the father and, without wasting another word, pointed with his index finger to Gregor, who was moving slowly forward. The violin fell silent, the gentleman in the middle first smiled at his friends, shaking his head, and then looked at Gregor again. The father seemed to think that, to begin with, it was more necessary to placate the lodgers than to chase away Gregor, even though the men were not at all excited and Gregor seemed to entertain them more than the violin playing. He ran over to them and, with arms outspread, he tried to make them withdraw into their room, at the same time blocking their view of Gregor with his body. Now they actually got a little sore; it was no longer possible to tell whether this was due to the father's behavior or to the realization now dawning on them that, without their knowledge, they had had a next-door neighbor like Gregor. They demanded explanations from the father, they themselves now raised their arms, they plucked uneasily at their beards, and only slowly retreated toward their room. Meanwhile the sister had gotten over the state of total absence that had come over her after the abruptly terminated performance; after she had held the violin and the bow for some time in her limply hanging hands and had continued to look at the music as if she were still playing, she had roused herself all at once; she had placed the instrument on the lap of her mother, who was still sitting on her chair gasping for breath, her lungs pumping violently, and had run into the adjoining room, which the lodgers were approaching more quickly now under pressure from the father. One could see the blankets and pillows on the beds fly up and arrange themselves neatly in the sister's skilled hands. Even before the gentlemen had reached their room, she had finished making the beds and slipped out. The father seemed once more so infected by his obstinacy that he forgot all the respect he after all owed his lodgers. All he did was crowd them and crowd them until, already in the doorway to the room, the gentleman in the middle stamped his foot resoundingly, thereby bringing the father to a halt. "I hereby announce," he said, raising his hand and looking around for the mother and sister as well, "that in view of the disgusting conditions prevailing in this apartment and family"—here he spat promptly on the floor—"I am giving up my room as of tomorrow morning. Naturally I won't pay a thing for the days that I've lived here, either; on the contrary, I'm going to think seriously about whether I shouldn't sue you—believe me, the proof wouldn't be hard to come by." He fell silent and looked straight ahead of him, as if he were expecting something. And, indeed, his two friends immediately chimed in with the words: "We're also leaving tomorrow." Thereupon he seized the door handle and slammed the door violently.

The father staggered to his chair with groping hands and let himself fall onto it; it looked as if he were stretching out for his customary evening nap, but the rapid nodding of his seemingly uncontrollable head showed that he was by no means asleep. Gregor had lain still the whole time on the same spot where the lodgers had detected him. The disappointment over the failure of his plan, but perhaps also the weakness caused by so much fasting, made it impossible for him to move. He was afraid that, almost as a certainty, everything would come tumbling down upon him at the very next moment; and he was waiting. Not even the violin startled him when it slipped from the mother's trembling fingers, fell off her lap and emitted a resounding note.

"Dear parents," the sister said, striking the table with her hand by way of preamble, "we can't go on like this. If you perhaps don't realize it, I do. In front of this monstrous creature I refuse to pronounce my brother's name, and therefore I merely say: we have to try to get rid of it. We've tried all that's humanly possible to take care of it and put up with it; I think no one can reproach us in the slightest."

"She's perfectly right," said the father to himself. The mother, who was still too short of breath, began to cough hollowly into the hand she held before her, with a crazed look in her eyes.

The sister ran over to the mother and held her forehead. The sister's words seemed to have helped the father collect his thoughts; he had sat up straight and was playing with his messenger's cap between the dishes that were still left on the table after the lodgers' supper; and from time to time he looked over at the motionless Gregor.

"We have to try to get rid of it," the sister now said to her father only, because the mother, with her coughing, couldn't hear anything; "eventually it'll kill both of you, I can see it coming. When people already have to work as hard as all of us, they can't stand this perpetual torment at home, as well. I can't any more." And she burst into such a violent fit of weeping that her tears rained down onto her mother's face, from which she wiped them away with mechanical movements of the hand.

"My child," said the father sympathetically and with noticeable comprehension, "what are we supposed to do?"

The sister merely shrugged her shoulders to indicate the perplexity that had now taken hold of her during her crying fit, in contrast to her earlier self-confidence.

"If he understood us," said the father half-questioningly; in the midst of her tears she shook her hand violently to indicate that that was out of the question.

"If he understood us," repeated the father and, closing his eyes, absorbed in his own mind the sister's conviction of that impossibility, "then perhaps we could reach an agreement with him. But, as it is —"

"It's got to go," called the sister, "that's the only remedy, Father. All you have to do is try to shake off the idea that that's Gregor. Our real misfortune comes from having believed it for so long. But how can it be Gregor? If it were Gregor, he would long since have realized that it's impossible for people to live side by side with an animal like that, and would have gone away of his own free will. Then we would have had no more brother, but we could go on living and honor his memory. But, as it is, this animal persecutes us, drives away our lodgers, and obviously wants to take over the whole apartment and make us sleep in the street. Just look, Father," she suddenly yelled, "he's starting again!" And, in a panic that Gregor couldn't understand at all, the sister even deserted her mother, literally hurling herself from her chair, as if she would rather sacrifice her mother than remain in Gregor's vicinity; she dashed behind her father, who, agitated solely by her behavior, also stood up and, as if protecting the sister, half-raised his arms in front of her.

But Gregor hadn't the slightest wish to frighten anyone, least of all his sister. He had merely started to turn around, in order to regain his room, and that was naturally conspicuous because in his ailing condition he could only execute those difficult turns with the aid of his head, raising it and bumping it on the floor many times. He stopped and looked around. His good intentions seemed to have been recognized; the panic had lasted only for a moment. Now they all looked at him in silent sorrow. The mother was slumped in her chair, her legs outstretched and pressed together; her eyes were almost closing with exhaustion; the father and sister were sitting side by side; the sister had placed her hand around the father's neck.

"Now perhaps I can turn around," thought Gregor, and resumed his labors. He was unable to suppress the heavy breathing caused by the exertion, and had to stop to rest from time to time. Otherwise, no one was rushing him, everything was left to him. When he had completed the turn, he immediately began to head back in a straight line. He was amazed at the great distance that separated him from his room, and couldn't comprehend how, feeling so weak, he had just a while before covered the same ground almost without noticing it. His mind being constantly bent on nothing but fast crawling, he scarcely paid attention to the fact that he was not being disturbed by any word or outcry from his family. Only when already in the doorway did he turn his head, not all the way, because he felt his neck growing stiff, but enough to see that nothing had changed behind him except that his sister had stood up. His last look was at his mother, who had fallen asleep completely.

Scarcely was he inside his room when the door was hastily closed, barred and locked. The sudden noise behind him scared Gregor so badly that his little legs buckled. It was his sister who had been in such a rush. She had already been standing there on her feet and waiting, then she had leaped forward with light steps — Gregor hadn't heard her approaching — and she called "At last!" to her parents as she turned the key in the lock.

"And now?" Gregor asked himself, and looked around in the darkness. He soon made the discovery that he could no longer move at all. This didn't surprise him; in fact, he found it unnatural that up until then he had actually been able to get around on those thin little legs. Besides, he felt relatively comfortable. True, he had pains all over his body, but he felt as if they were getting gradually milder and milder and would finally pass away altogether. By now he hardly felt the rotten apple in his back and the inflamed area around it, which were completely covered with soft dust. He recalled his family with affection and love. His opinion about the necessity for him to disappear was, if possible, even firmer than his sister's. He remained in this state of vacant and peaceful contemplation until the tower clock struck the third morning hour. He was still alive when the world started to become brighter outside the window. Then his head involuntarily sank down altogether, and his last breath issued faintly from his nostrils.

When the cleaning woman arrived early in the morning — in her natural strength and haste, despite frequent requests not to do so, she slammed all the doors so loud that throughout the apartment, from the moment she came, it was impossible to sleep peacefully — she found nothing out of the ordinary at first during her customary brief visit to Gregor. She thought he was lying motionless like that on purpose, acting insulted; she gave him credit for full reasoning powers. Because by chance she was carrying the long broom, she tried to tickle Gregor with it from her position in the doorway. When this proved fruitless, she became annoyed and jabbed Gregor a little, and only when she had moved him from the spot, without any resistance on his part, did she take notice. When she soon recognized the true state of affairs, she opened her eyes wide and gave a whistle, but didn't stay there long; instead, she tore open the bedroom door and shouted into the darkness: "Come take a look, it's croaked; it's lying there, a total goner."

The Samsas sat up in bed and were hard put to overcome the fright that the cleaning woman had given them until they finally grasped her announcement. Then Mr. and Mrs. Samsa got out of bed quickly, each on his side; Mr. Samsa threw the blanket over his shoulders, Mrs. Samsa came out wearing only her nightgown; in this way they entered Gregor's room. Meanwhile the parlor door had also opened; Grete had been sleeping there since the lodgers moved in; she was fully dressed as if she hadn't slept at all; the pallor of her face seemed to indicate that, too. "Dead?" asked Mrs. Samsa, and looked up questioningly at the cleaning woman, even though she was able to examine everything herself and could recognize it even without any examination. "I'll say!" replied the cleaning woman, and, as a proof, pushed Gregor's corpse another long way to the side with her broom. Mrs. Samsa made a motion as if to restrain the broom, but didn't do so. "Well," said Mr. Samsa, "now we can thank God." He crossed himself, and the three women followed his example. Grete, who didn't take her eyes off the corpse, said: "Just look how thin he was. Yes, he hadn't been eating anything for so long. The food came out of his room just the way it went in." Indeed, Gregor's body was completely flat and dry; actually that could be seen only now, when he was no longer lifted up on his little legs and nothing else diverted their attention.

"Come into our room for a while, Grete," said Mrs. Samsa with a melancholy smile, and, not without looking back at the corpse, Grete followed her parents into their bedroom. The cleaning woman shut the door and opened the window all the way. Despite the early morning hour, the fresh air already had a warm feeling to it. For by now it was the end of March.

The three lodgers stepped out of their room and, in amazement, looked around for their breakfast; the family had forgotten it. "Where's breakfast?!" the gentleman in the middle grumpily asked the cleaning woman. But she put her finger to her lips and then hastily and silently beckoned to the gentlemen to come into Gregor's room. They did so, and then, with their hands in the pockets of their somewhat shabby jackets, they stood around Gregor's corpse in the now completely bright room.

Then the bedroom door opened, and Mr. Samsa appeared in his uniform, with his wife on one arm and his daughter on the other. All of them had obviously been weeping; from time to time Grete pressed her face against her father's arm.

"Leave my home at once!" said Mr. Samsa, and pointed to the door, without freeing himself from the women. "What do you mean?" said the gentleman in the middle, somewhat taken aback, and put on a saccharine smile. The two others kept their hands behind their backs, rubbing them together uninterruptedly, as if in joyous anticipation of a major quarrel, which had to come out in their favor. "I mean exactly what I say," Mr. Samsa answered, and, with his two female companions, moved in a direct line toward the lodger. The latter stood still at first, looking at the floor, as if all the ideas in his head were being rearranged. "In that case, we're going," he then said, looking up at Mr. Samsa, as if, with a humility that was suddenly setting in, he were requesting new permission even for that decision. Mr. Samsa merely gave him a few brief nods, his eyes glaring. Thereupon the gentleman did indeed immediately take long strides into the hallway; his two friends, who for a while now had been listening with their hands completely at rest, now practically leaped after him, as if fearing that Mr. Samsa might enter the hall before them and cut off the liaison with their leader. In the hallway, all three took their hats off the hooks, drew their walking sticks out of the walking-stick stand, bowed in silence and left the apartment. With a mistrust that proved to be totally unjustified, Mr. Samsa and the two women stepped out onto the landing; leaning against the railing, they watched the three gentlemen descend the long staircase slowly but steadily, disappear on each floor into the same bend of the stairwell, and emerge again after a few moments; the lower they got, the more the Samsa family lost interest in them, and when a butcher boy, proudly bearing his tray on his head, met up with them and then climbed the stairs far above them, Mr. Samsa and the women left the railing, and they all returned to their apartment as if they were relieved.

They decided to spend that day resting and strolling; they not only deserved that pause from work, they absolutely needed it. And so they sat down at the table and wrote three letters of excuse, Mr. Samsa to the bank directors, Mrs. Samsa to the people who gave her piecework and Grete to her employer. While they were writing, the cleaning woman came in to say she was leaving because her morning chores were done. At first the three writers merely nodded, without looking up; it was only when the cleaning woman made no signs of going that they looked up in annoyance. "Well?" asked Mr. Samsa. The cleaning woman stood in the doorway smiling, as if she had a message that would make the family tremendously happy but would only deliver it if they questioned her thoroughly. The almost vertical little ostrich feather on her hat, which had annoyed Mr. Samsa all the time she'd been working for them, was waving slightly in all directions. "Well, what is it you want?" asked Mrs. Samsa, for whom the cleaning woman still had the most respect. "Yes," answered the cleaning woman, whose friendly laughter prevented her from continuing right away, "you don't have to worry your heads about how to clear out that trash next door. It's all taken care of." Mrs. Samsa and Grete lowered their heads to their letters, as if they wanted to go on writing; Mr. Samsa, who perceived that the cleaning woman now wanted to start describing everything in detail, forbade that decisively with an upheld hand. Now that she wasn't able to deliver a narration, she recalled the big hurry she was in; shouted, obviously peeved, "So long, one and all!"; turned on her heels furiously and left the apartment, slamming every door thunderously.

"We'll discharge her tonight," said Mr. Samsa, but received no reply from either his wife or his daughter, since the cleaning woman seemed to have once more disturbed the peace of mind they had just barely attained. They got up, went over to the window and stayed there, their arms around each other. Mr. Samsa turned around toward them on his chair and watched them silently for a while. Then he called: "Oh, come on over. Let bygones be bygones now. And have a little consideration for me, too." The women obeyed him at once, rushed over to him, caressed him and finished their letters quickly.

Then all three of them left the apartment together, something they hadn't done for months, and took the trolley out to the country on the edge of town. The car, in which they were the only passengers, was brightly lit by the warm sun. Leaning back comfortably on their seats, they discussed their prospects for the future, and it proved that, on closer examination, these were not at all bad, because the jobs that all three had, but which they hadn't really asked one another about before, were thoroughly advantageous and particularly promising for later on. Naturally the greatest immediate improvement in their situation would result easily from a change of apartment; now they would take a smaller and cheaper, but better located and in general more practical, apartment than their present one, which Gregor had found for them. While they were conversing in this way, Mr. and Mrs. Samsa, looking at their daughter, who was becoming more lively all the time, realized at almost the very same moment that recently, in spite of all the cares that had made her cheeks pale, she had blossomed out into a beautiful, well-built girl. Becoming more silent and almost unconsciously communicating with each other by looks, they thought it was now time to find a good husband for her. And they took it as a confirmation of their new dreams and good intentions when, at the end of their ride, their daughter stood up first and stretched her young body.

In the Penal Colony

"IT'S A MACHINE like no other," said the officer to the explorer, as he surveyed the machine with a somewhat admiring look, although he was so familiar with it. The explorer seemed to have accepted merely out of courtesy when the governor had invited him to attend the execution of a soldier condemned to death for disobeying and insulting his superior. Even in the penal colony there was no particularly great interest in this execution. At any rate, here in the deep, sandy little valley enclosed on all sides by bare slopes, the only people present, apart from the officer and the explorer, were the condemned man, a dull-witted, wide-mouthed fellow with ungroomed hair and face, and a soldier, who held the heavy chain that gathered together all the small chains with which the condemned man was fettered at his wrists, ankles and neck, and which were also connected to one another by intermediate chains. Anyway, the condemned man had a look of such doglike devotion that you might picture him being allowed to run around at liberty on the slopes and returning at the beginning of the execution if you just whistled for him.

The explorer had little taste for the machine and walked back and forth behind the condemned man with an almost visible lack of concern, while the officer saw to the final preparations, now crawling under the machine, which was sunk deep into the ground, now climbing a ladder to inspect the upper sections. Those were tasks that could really have been left to a mechanic, but the officer performed them with great enthusiasm, either because he was a special devotee of this machine or because, for some other reasons, the work couldn't be entrusted to anyone else. "All ready now," he finally called, and climbed down the ladder. He was unusually exhausted, breathed with his mouth wide open, and had two delicate lady's handkerchiefs crammed behind the collar of his uniform. "These uniforms are surely too heavy for the tropics," said the explorer, instead of inquiring about the machine, as the officer had expected. "Of course," said the officer, washing the oil and grease off his hands in a bucket that stood ready there, "but they represent our homeland; we don't want to be cut off from our country. — But now you see this machine," he added without a pause, drying his hands on a cloth and simultaneously pointing to the machine. "Up to this point some hand operations were still necessary; from this point on, however, the machine does all the work by itself." The explorer nodded and followed the officer. The latter, attempting to insure himself against all incidents, said: "Naturally, disorders occur; true, I hope none will happen today, but they still have to be reckoned with. You see, the machine needs to keep going for twelve hours uninterruptedly. But if disorders do occur, they will be very minor and will be cleared away at once."

"Won't you have a seat?" he finally asked, pulling a cane-bottomed chair out from a stack of them and offering it to the explorer, who couldn't refuse. He was now sitting on the rim of a pit, into which he cast a fleeting glance. It wasn't very deep. On one side of the pit the excavated earth was heaped up into a mound, on the other side stood the machine. "I don't know," said the officer, "whether the governor has already explained the machine to you." The explorer made a vague sign with his hand; the officer asked for nothing better, for now he could explain the machine himself. "This machine," he said, grasping a cranking rod, on which he supported himself, "is an invention of our previous governor. I participated in the very first experiments and took part in all the other developments until it was perfected. Of course, the credit for the invention is due to him alone. Have you heard about our previous governor? No? Well, I'm not claiming too much when I say that the organization of the entire penal colony is his creation. We, his friends, already knew at the time of his death that his plan for the colony was so perfectly worked out that his successor, even if he had a thousand new schemes in mind, wouldn't be able to change the old arrangements for many years, at least. And our prediction came true; the new governor had to acknowledge it. Too bad you never met the previous governor! — But," the officer interrupted himself, "I'm babbling, and his machine is here before us. It consists, as you see, of three parts. In the course of time each of these parts has acquired a somewhat popular nickname. The lowest one is called the bed, the highest one is called the sketcher and this central, freely hanging part is called the harrow." "The harrow?" the explorer asked. He hadn't been listening too attentively, the sunlight had lodged itself all too strongly in the shadeless valley, it was hard to gather one's thoughts. And so he considered the officer all the more admirable, seeing him in his tight parade jacket, laden with epaulets and covered with braid, expounding his subject with such enthusiasm and, what's more, still busying himself at a screw here and there, while speaking, screwdriver in hand. The soldier seemed to be of the same frame of mind as the explorer. He had wrapped the condemned man's chain around both wrists, and was leaning on his rifle with one hand; his head was sunk on his chest and he was totally unconcerned. The explorer wasn't surprised at this, because the officer was speaking French, and surely neither the soldier nor the condemned man understood French. Which made it all the more curious that the condemned man was nevertheless making an effort to follow the officer's explanation. With a kind of sleepy persistence he always directed his gaze to the spot the officer was pointing out at the moment, and when the latter was now interrupted by a question from the explorer, he, too, as well as the officer, looked at the explorer.

"Yes, the harrow," said the officer, "the name fits. The needles are arranged in harrow fashion, and the whole thing is manipulated like a harrow, although it remains in one place only, and works much more artistically. Anyway, you'll understand it right away. The condemned man is laid here on the bed. — I'm going to describe the machine first, you see, and only after that will I have the procedure itself carried out. Then you'll be better able to follow it. Besides, one cogwheel in the sketcher is worn too smooth, and squeaks a lot when in operation; when that's going on, it's barely possible to understand one another; unfortunately, spare parts are very hard to procure here. — So then, here is the bed, as I was saying. It's completely covered by a layer of absorbent cotton; you'll soon learn the purpose of that. The condemned man is placed stomach down on this cotton, naked, naturally; here are straps for his hands, here for his feet, here for his neck, to buckle him in tight. Here at the head end of the bed, where, as I said, the man's face lies at first, there is this little felt projection, which can easily be adjusted so that it pops right into the man's mouth. Its purpose is to keep him from screaming and chewing up his tongue. Naturally, the man is forced to put the felt in his mouth or else his neck would be broken by the neck strap." "This is absorbent cotton?" the explorer asked, bending forward. "Yes, of course," said the officer with a smile, "feel it yourself." He took the explorer's hand and ran it over the bed. "It's a specially prepared absorbent cotton, that's why it's so hard to recognize; as I continue talking, I'll get to its purpose." The explorer was now a little more interested in the machine; shading his eyes from the sun with his hand, he looked up at the top of the machine. It was a large construction. The bed and the sketcher were of the same size and looked like two dark trunks for clothing. The sketcher was installed about six feet above the bed; the two were connected at the corners by four brass rods, which were practically darting rays in the sunlight. Between the trunks the harrow hung freely on a steel ribbon.

The officer had scarcely noticed the explorer's earlier indifference, but he was fully aware of the interest he was now beginning to feel, so he ceased his exposition in order to give the explorer time to observe unmolestedly. The condemned man mimicked the explorer; since he couldn't raise his hand to his brow, he blinked upward with unshaded eyes.

"Well, then, the man lies there," said the explorer, leaning back in his chair and crossing his legs.

"Yes," said the officer, pushing his cap back a bit and drawing his hand over his hot face. "Now listen! The bed and the sketcher each has its own electric battery; the bed needs it for itself, the sketcher needs it for the harrow. As soon as the man is strapped in tight, the bed is set in motion. It vibrates in tiny, very rapid jerks sideways and up and down at the same time. You may have seen similar machines in sanatoriums, but in our bed all the movements are precisely calculated; you see, they have to be scrupulously synchronized with the movements of the harrow. It is this harrow, however, that actually carries out the sentence."

"What *is* the sentence?" the explorer asked. "You don't know that, either?" said the officer in amazement, biting his lips: "Forgive me if my explanations may appear haphazard; I ask your pardon most humbly. You see, in the past the governor used to give the explanations; but the new governor has exempted himself from the honor of this duty; but that even such a distinguished visitor" — the explorer attempted to forestall this praise with a gesture of both hands, but the officer insisted on the expression — "that he doesn't apprise even such a distinguished visitor of the form of our sentence, is another innovation that — " He had an oath on his lips, but controlled himself and merely said: "I wasn't notified of that, it's no fault of mine. Anyway, I am the one best capable of explaining our types of sentence, because I carry here" — he tapped his breast pocket — "the designs drawn by the previous governor bearing on the matter."

"Designs by the governor himself?" asked the explorer. "Was he a combination of everything, then? Was he a soldier, judge, engineer, chemist and designer?"

"Yes, indeed," said the officer, nodding, his gaze fixed and meditative. Then he looked at his hands searchingly; he didn't consider them clean enough to touch the drawings, so he went over to the bucket and washed them again. Then he pulled out a little leather wallet, saying: "Our sentence isn't severe. The regulation that the condemned man has broken is written on his body with the harrow. This condemned man, for example" — the officer pointed to the man — "will have 'Honor your superior!' written on his body."

The explorer glanced fleetingly at the man; when the officer had pointed to him, he had been standing with lowered head, seeming to concentrate all his powers of hearing in order to find out something. But the movements of his lips, which bulged as he compressed them, clearly showed he couldn't understand a thing. The explorer had wanted to ask this and that, but now, looking at the man, he merely asked: "Does he know his sentence?" "No," said the officer, and wanted to continue his exposition at once, but the explorer interrupted him: "He doesn't know his own sentence?" "No," the officer said again, then stopped short for a moment, as if desiring the explorer to offer some substantial reason for his question, and then said: "It would be pointless to inform him of it. After all, he'll learn it on his body." The explorer was now ready to remain silent, when he felt the condemned man turn his eyes toward him; he seemed to be asking whether he could approve of the procedure that had been described. And so the explorer, who had already leaned back, bent forward again and asked another question: "But he does at least know, doesn't he, that he has been condemned?" "Not that, either," said the officer, and smiled at the explorer, as if he were still expecting a few more peculiar utterances from him. "No," said the explorer, rubbing his forehead, "and so even now the man still doesn't know how his defense was received?" "He had no opportunity to defend himself," said the officer, looking off to the side, as if he were talking to himself and didn't wish to embarrass the explorer by telling him what was so obvious to himself. "But he must have had an opportunity to defend himself," said the explorer, rising from his chair.

The officer realized he was running the risk of being delayed for a long time in the explanation of the machine; so he went over to the explorer, locked his arm in his, pointed to the condemned man, who, now that their attention was so clearly directed toward him, straightened up smartly — the soldier also pulled the chain taut — and said: "The matter is as follows. Here in the penal colony I serve as a judge. Despite my youth. Because in all penal matters I stood side by side with the previous governor, and I also know the machine best. The principle behind my decisions is: Guilt is always beyond doubt. Other courts can't adhere to this principle, because they consist of several judges and have even higher courts over them. That isn't the case here, or at least it wasn't under the previous governor. To be sure, the new one has already shown a desire to meddle with my court, but so far I've managed to fend him off, and I'll continue to manage it. — You wanted an explanation of this case; it's just as simple as all of them. This morning a captain reported that this man, who's assigned to him as an orderly and sleeps in front of his door, slept through his tour of duty. You see, he is obliged to get up every hour on the hour and salute in front of the captain's door. Certainly not an onerous duty, but a necessary one, since he has to stay alert as both a guard and a servant. Last night the captain wanted to verify whether his orderly was doing his duty. At the stroke of two he opened his door and found him curled up asleep. He went for his riding whip and struck him on the face. Now, instead of standing up and asking for forgiveness, the man grasped his master by the legs, shook him and shouted: "Hey, throw away that whip or I'll gobble you up." Those are the facts of the matter. An hour ago the captain came to me, I wrote down his declaration and followed it up with the sentence. Then I had the man put in chains. All that was very simple. If I had first summoned the man and interrogated him, that would only have led to confusion. He would have lied; if I had succeeded in disproving those lies, he would have replaced them with new lies, and so on. But, as it is, I've got him and I won't let go of him again. — Does that now explain everything? But time is passing, the execution ought to begin by now, and I'm not finished yet with the explanation of the machine." He urged the explorer to sit down again, stepped up to the machine once more, and began: "As you see, the shape of the harrow corresponds to the human form; here is the harrow for the upper part of the body, here are the harrows for the legs. For the head there is only this small spike. Is that clear to you?" He leaned over to the explorer in a friendly way, ready to give the most comprehensive explanations.

The explorer looked at the harrow with furrowed brow. The information about the judicial procedure had left him unsatisfied. All the same, he had to tell himself that this was, after all, a penal colony, that special regulations were required here, and that a military code had to be followed, even to extreme limits. But, in addition, he placed some hope in the new governor, who obviously, if only slowly, intended to introduce a new procedure that couldn't penetrate this officer's thick head. Pursuing this train of thought, the explorer asked: "Will the governor attend the execution?" "It's uncertain," said the officer, touched on a sore spot by the blunt question, and his friendly expression clouded over: "For that very reason we must make haste. In fact, as sorry as that makes me, I must shorten my explanations. But tomorrow, when the machine has been cleaned again — its getting so very dirty is its only shortcoming — I could fill in the smaller details. And so, for now, only the most essential facts. — When the man is lying on the bed and the bed begins to vibrate, the harrow lowers itself onto the body. It adjusts itself in such a manner that it just barely touches the body with its sharp points; once this adjustment is completed, this steel cable immediately stiffens into a rod. And now the machine goes into play. An uninitiated person notices no outward difference in the punishments. The harrow seems to work in a uniform way. Quivering, it jabs its points into the body, which is already shaken by the bed. Now, to allow everybody to inspect the execution of the sentence, the harrow was made of glass. Several technical difficulties had to be overcome to embed the needles in it firmly, but we succeeded after a number of experiments. We literally spared no effort. And now everyone can watch through the glass and see how the inscription on the body is done. Won't you step closer and take a look at the needles?"

The explorer got up slowly, went over and bent over the harrow. "Here," said the officer, "you see two types of needles in a complex arrangement. Each long one has a short one next to it. You see, the long ones do the writing and the short ones squirt water to wash away the blood and to keep the lettering clear at all times. The bloody water is then channeled here into small grooves and finally runs off into this main groove, whose drainpipe leads into the pit." With one finger the officer indicated the precise route the bloody water had to take. When, in order to give the most graphic demonstration, he made the actual motion of catching it in his two hands at the outlet of the drainpipe, the explorer raised his head and, groping backwards with his hand, attempted to regain his chair. Then he saw, to his horror, that, like him, the condemned man had accepted the officer's invitation to take a close look at the structure of the harrow. He had tugged the drowsy soldier forward a little by the chain and had also stooped over the glass. He could be seen searching with unsure eyes for what the two gentlemen had just been observing, but not succeeding for lack of the explanation. He bent over this way and that way. Again and again he ran his eyes over the glass. The explorer wanted to drive him back, because he was probably committing a punishable offense. But the officer restrained the explorer firmly with one hand, and with the other took a clod of earth from the mound and threw it at the soldier. The latter raised his eyes with a start, saw what the condemned man had dared to do, dropped his rifle, dug his heels into the ground, tore the condemned man back so hard that he fell right over, and then looked down at the writhing man, who was making his chains rattle. "Pick him up!" shouted the officer, because he noticed that the explorer's attention was being distracted far too much by the condemned man. The explorer even leaned forward all the way across the harrow, not caring about it at all, concerned only to discover what was happening to the condemned man. "Handle him carefully!" shouted the officer again. He ran around the machine, seized the condemned man under the arms himself, and, with the aid of the soldier, raised him to his feet, although the man's feet slid out from under him several times.

"By now I know everything," said the explorer when the officer came back to him. "Except for the most important thing of all," the latter said, grasping the explorer's arm and pointing upward: "Up there in the sketcher are the cogwheels that regulate the motion of the harrow, and those wheels are pre-set in accordance with the pattern called for by the sentence. I am still using the previous governor's designs. Here they are"—he drew a few sheets out of the leather wallet—"but unfortunately I cannot hand them to you; they're the most precious things I possess. Sit down, I'll show them to you from this distance, then you'll be able to see them all clearly." He showed the first sheet. The explorer would gladly have made some appreciative remark, but all he saw was mazelike lines in complicated crisscrosses, covering the paper so completely that it was hard to see the white spaces between them. "Read it," said the officer. "I can't," said the explorer. "But it's legible," said the officer. "It's very artistic," said the explorer evasively, "but I can't decipher it." "Yes," said the officer, laughed and pocketed the wallet again, "it isn't model calligraphy for schoolboys. One has to study it a long time. Even you would surely recognize it finally. Naturally, it can't be any simple script; you see, it is not supposed to kill at once, but only after a period of twelve hours on the average; the turning point is calculated to occur during the sixth hour. And so there must be many, many ornaments surrounding the actual letters; the real message encircles the body only within a narrow band; the rest of the body is set aside for the decorations. Are you now able to appreciate the work of the harrow and of the whole machine?—Look!" He leaped onto the ladder, turned a wheel and called down: "Careful, step to one side!" and everything went into action. If the cogwheel hadn't been squeaking, it would have been magnificent. As if the officer were surprised by that disturbing wheel, he threatened it with his fist, then, excusing himself, extended his arms toward the explorer and climbed down hastily in order to observe the operation of the machine from below. There was still something out of order which only he noticed; he climbed up again, thrust both hands into the sketcher, then, to get down more quickly, slid down one of the rods instead of using the ladder, and now, to make himself heard over the noise, shouted with extreme tension into the explorer's ear. "Do you understand the process? The harrow begins to write; when it is finished with the first draft of the lettering on the man's back, the layer of absorbent cotton rolls and turns the body slowly onto its side to give the harrow additional space. Meanwhile the areas that are pierced by the writing press against the cotton, which, thanks to its special preparation, stops the bleeding at once and clears the way for the lettering to sink in further. The prongs here at the edge of the harrow then rip the cotton from the wounds as the body continues to turn, fling it into the pit, and the harrow can go on working. In this way it writes more and more deeply for the twelve hours. For the first six hours the condemned man lives almost as he previously did, but suffering pain. After two hours the felt is removed, because the man has no more strength to scream. In this electrically heated bowl at the head end we place hot boiled rice and milk, from which the man, if he feels like it, can take whatever he can get hold of with his tongue. None of them passes up the opportunity. I know of none, and my experience is extensive. Only around the sixth hour does he lose his pleasure in eating. Then I generally kneel down here and observe this phenomenon. The man seldom swallows the last mouthful, he just turns it around in his mouth and spits it out into the pit. Then I have to duck or he'll hit me in the face with it. But then, how quiet the man becomes around the sixth hour! Even the dumbest one starts to understand. It begins around the eyes. From there it spreads out. A sight that could tempt someone to lie down alongside the man under the harrow. Nothing further happens, the man merely begins to decipher the writing; he purses his lips as if listening to something. As you've seen, it isn't easy to decipher the script with your eyes; but our man deciphers it with his wounds. True, it takes a lot of effort; he needs six hours to complete it. But then the harrow skewers him completely and throws him into the pit, where he splashes down into the bloody water and the cotton. Then the execution is over, and we, the soldier and I, bury him."

The explorer had inclined his ear toward the officer and, his hands in his jacket pockets, was watching the machine run. The condemned man was watching it, too, but without understanding. He was stooping a little and following the moving needles, when the soldier, at a sign from the officer, cut through his shirt and trousers in the back with a knife, so that they fell off the condemned man; he wanted to make a grab for the falling garments, in order to hide his nakedness, but the soldier lifted him up in the air and shook the last scraps off him. The officer turned off the machine, and in the silence that ensued the condemned man was placed under the harrow. His chains were removed and replaced by the fastened straps; at the first moment this seemed to be almost a relief for the condemned man. And now the harrow lowered itself a little more, because he was a thin man. When the points touched him, a shudder ran over his skin; while the soldier was busy with his right hand, he stretched out the left, without knowing in what direction; but it was toward the spot where the explorer was standing. The officer uninterruptedly watched the explorer from the side, as if trying to read in his face the impression being made on him by the execution, which he had now explained to him at least superficially.

The strap intended for the wrist tore; probably the soldier had drawn it up too tightly. The officer was to help, the soldier showed him the torn-off piece of strap. And the officer did go over to him, saying: "The machine is composed of many, many parts; from time to time something has to rip or break; but that shouldn't falsify one's total judgment. Besides, an immediate substitute is available for the strap; I shall use a chain; of course, for the right arm the delicacy of the vibrations will be impaired." And, while he attached the chains, he added: "The means for maintaining the machine are now quite limited. Under the previous governor there was a fund, readily accessible to me, set aside for just that purpose. There was a supply depot here in which all conceivable spare parts were stored. I confess, I was almost wasteful with it, I mean in the past, not now, as the new governor claims; for him everything serves as a mere pretext for combating the old arrangements. Now he has the machine fund under his own management, and, if I send for a new strap, the torn one is requested as evidence, the new one doesn't come for ten days, and then is of poorer quality and isn't worth much. But how I am supposed to run the machine in the meantime without a strap — nobody cares about that."

The explorer thought it over: It's always a ticklish thing to interfere in someone else's affairs in some decisive way. He was neither a citizen of the penal colony nor a citizen of the country it belonged to. If he wished to condemn the execution or even prevent it, they could say to him: "You're a foreigner, keep quiet." He would have no reply to that, but would only be able to add that in this case he didn't even understand his own motives, since he was traveling purely with the intention of seeing things, and by no means that of altering other people's legal codes, or the like. But matters here were truly very tempting. The injustice of the proceedings and the inhumanity of the execution couldn't be denied. No one could assume that the traveler was doing anything self-serving, because the condemned man was unknown to him, not a compatriot and in no way a person who elicited sympathy. The explorer himself had letters of recommendation from high official sources, he had been welcomed here with great courtesy, and the fact that he had been invited to this execution even seemed to indicate that his opinion of this court was desired. Moreover, this was all the more likely since the governor, as he had now heard more than explicitly, was not partial to these proceedings and was almost hostile to the officer.

At that point the explorer heard the officer shout with rage. He had just shoved the felt gag into the condemned man's mouth, not without difficulty, when the condemned man shut his eyes with an uncontrollable urge to vomit, and vomited. Hastily the officer pulled him up and away from the gag, trying to turn his head toward the pit; but it was too late, the filth was already running down the machine. "All the governor's fault!" yelled the officer, beside himself, shaking the brass rods in front, "my machine is getting befouled like a stable." With trembling hands he showed the explorer what had happened. "Haven't I tried for hours on end to get it across to the governor that no more food is to be given a day before the execution? But the new, lenient school of thought is of a different opinion. The governor's ladies stuff the man's mouth with sweets before he's led away. All his life he's lived on stinking fish and now he's got to eat sweets! But it would still be possible, I'd have no objection, if they only supplied me with a new piece of felt, which I've been requesting for three months now. How can anyone put this felt in his mouth without being disgusted, after more than a hundred men have sucked on it and bitten it while they were dying?"

The condemned man had put his head down and looked peaceful, the soldier was busy cleaning the machine with the condemned man's shirt. The officer walked over to the explorer, who with some sort of foreboding took a step backwards, but the officer took him by the hand and drew him to one side. "I want to say a few words to you in confidence," he said; "that is, if I may?" "Of course," said the explorer, and then listened with lowered eyes.

"This procedure and this execution, which you now have the opportunity to admire, are no long openly supported by any one in our colony at the present time. I am their only spokesman, and at the same time the only spokesman for the old governor's legacy. I can no longer contemplate a further extension of the procedure; I consume all my strength to retain what still exists. While the old governor was alive, the colony was full of his followers; I have some of the old governor's power of persuasion, but I lack his authority entirely; as a consequence, his followers have gone underground; there are still a lot of them, but none of them will admit it. If today — that is, on an execution day — you go into the teahouse and keep your ears open, you will perhaps hear nothing but ambiguous utterances. They are all loyal followers, but under the present governor, with his present views, I can't use them at all. And now I ask you. Is it right that, on account of this governor and his women, who influence him, a life's work like this" — he pointed to the machine — "should be wrecked? Is that to be allowed? Even if someone is a foreigner and only staying on our island for a few days? But there's no time to be lost, preparations are under way to combat my jurisdiction; meetings are already being held in the governor's office in which I am not asked to participate; even your visit today seems to me to be characteristic of the whole situation; they're cowardly and send you, a foreigner, out in advance. — How different the execution was in the old times! A day before the punishment was meted out, the whole valley was already crammed with people; they all came only to watch; early in the morning the governor would arrive with his ladies; fanfares roused the whole encampment; I reported that all was in readiness; the guests — no high official was allowed to be absent — grouped themselves around the machine; this stack of cane-bottomed chairs is a pathetic survival from those days. The machine was freshly polished and gleaming; for almost every execution I put in new spare parts. In front of hundreds of eyes — all the spectators stood on their toes all the way up to the heights there — the condemned man was placed under the harrow by the governor himself. What a private soldier is allowed to do today, was then my task, the chief judge's, and was an honor for me. And now the execution began! No false note disturbed the operation of the machine. At this point many people were no longer watching, but were lying on the sand with closed eyes; everybody knew: Now justice will be done. In the silence all that could be heard was the condemned man's sighing, muffled by the felt. Today the machine no longer manages to squeeze a sigh out of the condemned man that's loud enough not to be stifled by the felt; but in those days the writing needles exuded a corrosive fluid that isn't allowed to be used any more. Well, and then the sixth hour arrived! It was impossible to comply with everyone's request to watch from up close. The governor in his wisdom ordered that the children should be considered first and foremost; of course, thanks to my station, I was always allowed to stay right there; often I would squat down, holding two small children in my arms, right and left. How we all captured the transfigured expression on the tortured face, how we held our cheeks in the glow of this finally achieved and already perishing justice! What times those were, my friend!" The officer had obviously forgotten who was in front of him; he had embraced the explorer and had laid his head on his shoulder. The explorer felt extremely awkward, and impatiently looked past the officer. The soldier had finished his cleaning and had just poured boiled rice into the bowl from a jar. The condemned man, who seemed to have recovered completely by this time, had scarcely noticed this when he began snatching at the rice with his tongue. The soldier kept pushing him away again, because the rice was meant for a later time, but surely the soldier also was acting improperly when he dug into the rice with his dirty hands and ate some before the eyes of the covetous condemned man.

The officer quickly regained control of himself. "Please don't think I wanted to play on your sympathy," he said, "I know it's impossible to make anyone understand those times today. Anyway, the machine is still working and speaks for itself. It speaks for itself even when left alone in this valley. And at the end the corpse still falls into the pit with that incomprehensibly gentle sweep, even if hundreds of people are no longer clustered around the pit like flies, as in the past. Then we had to install a strong railing around the pit; it was torn down long ago."

The explorer wanted to move his face out of the officer's gaze, and looked around aimlessly. The officer thought he was contemplating the barrenness of the valley; and so he took his hands, stepped around him to make their eyes meet, and asked: "Do you observe the disgrace?"

But the explorer remained silent. For a while the officer let him alone; with legs planted far apart, his hands on his hips, he stood quietly looking at the ground. Then he smiled at the explorer encouragingly and said: "I was near you yesterday when the governor invited you. I heard the invitation. I know the governor. I immediately understood his purpose in inviting you. Even though his authority may be great enough for him to take steps against me, he still doesn't dare to, but instead he wishes to expose me to your opinion, that of a highly esteemed foreign visitor. He worked it out carefully; this is your second day on the island, you didn't know the old governor and his philosophy, you are prejudiced by European points of view, perhaps you are an opponent on principle of any kind of capital punishment, and of this kind of execution by machine in particular; furthermore, you observe that the execution is performed without the participation of the public, in a dismal atmosphere, on a machine that is already somewhat damaged — now, taking all this together, thinks the governor, wouldn't it be quite possible for you to consider my procedure incorrect? And if you consider it incorrect (I'm still stating the governor's train of thought), you won't keep silent about it, because you must surely trust your tried-and-true convictions. Of course, you've seen and learned to respect many peculiar customs of many nations, and so probably you won't come out against the procedure as openly as you might do at home. But the governor doesn't need that much. A hasty word, merely a careless word, is enough. It doesn't have to be rooted in your convictions, if only it apparently suits his purposes. I'm sure he's going to question you as shrewdly as possible. And his ladies will sit around in a circle, pricking up their ears; you'll say something like 'In our country the judicial procedure is different' or 'In our country the defendant is interrogated before the sentence' or 'In our country there are punishments other than capital punishment' or 'In our country torture was used only in the Middle Ages.' Those are all remarks that are just as correct as they seem self-evident to you, innocent remarks that do not impugn my procedure. But how will the governor take them? I can see him, the good governor, immediately pushing his chair aside and dashing onto the balcony, I can see his ladies pouring after him, I can now hear his voice — his ladies call it a voice of thunder — as he says: 'A great Occidental explorer, sent to investigate judicial procedure all over the world, has just said that our old traditional procedure is inhumane. After this judgment by such a personality, it is naturally impossible for me to tolerate this procedure any longer. As of this date, therefore, I decree — and so on.' You will want to intervene, you didn't say what he is proclaiming, you didn't call my procedure inhumane; on the contrary, in accordance with your profoundest insight, you consider it the most humane and the most fitting for human society, you also admire this machinery — but it's too late; you can't get onto the balcony, which is already full of ladies; you want to call attention to yourself; you want to shout; but a lady's hand shuts your mouth — and I and the achievement of the old governor are lost."

The explorer had to suppress a smile; the task he had considered so hard was thus so easy. He said evasively: "You overestimate my influence; the governor read my letter of recommendation, he knows I'm not an expert on judicial procedure. If I were to express an opinion, it would be the opinion of a private person, no more significant than anyone else's opinion, and at any rate much more insignificant than the opinion of the governor, who, if I'm not misinformed, has very wide-ranging powers in this penal colony. If his opinion of this procedure is as unshakable as you believe, then I'm afraid the end of this procedure has come anyway, without the need of my modest cooperation."

Did the officer understand by this time? No, he still didn't understand. He shook his head vigorously, cast a brief glance back at the condemned man and the soldier, who winced and left the rice alone; then he stepped up close to the explorer, looking not at his face but at a random area of his jacket, and said, more softly than before: "You don't know the governor; to some extent — please forgive the expression — you're an innocent in comparison with him and all of us; believe me, your influence cannot be rated highly enough. In fact, I was overjoyed when I heard that you were to attend the execution alone. That order of the governor's was directed against me, but now I'm turning it around in my favor. Undistracted by false insinuations and contemptuous glances — which couldn't have been avoided if more people had participated in the execution — you have listened to my explanations, you have seen the machine and you are now about to view the execution. Certainly your opinion has been formed; if some small uncertainties still persist, the sight of the execution will remove them. And now I request of you: help me in my dealings with the governor!"

The explorer wouldn't let him continue. "How could I?" he exclaimed, "it's altogether impossible. I can't help you any more than I can harm you."

"Yes, you can," said the officer. With some alarm the explorer saw that the officer was clenching his fists. "Yes, you can," the officer repeated even more urgently. "I have a plan that can't fail. You think your influence isn't enough. I know that it *is* enough. But even granting that you're right, isn't it still necessary to try everything, even measures that are inadequate, in order to preserve this procedure? So listen to my plan. To carry it out, it's necessary above all for you to conceal your opinion of the procedure as much as possible in the colony today. If you're not actually asked, you must by no means make a statement; but if you do make statements, they must be brief and vague; people should notice that it's hard for you to talk about it, that you're bitter, that, in case you were to speak openly, you would actually break out into curses. I'm not asking you to lie; not a bit; you should merely make brief replies, such as 'Yes, I saw the execution' or 'Yes, I heard all the explanations.' Only that, nothing more. Of course, there's enough reason for the resentment that people must see in you, even if it's not in the way the governor thinks. Naturally, he will misunderstand it completely and interpret it in his own fashion. That's the basis of my plan. Tomorrow in the government building, under his chairmanship, a big meeting of all the top administration officials will take place. Naturally, the governor has managed to turn such meetings into a show. A gallery has been built that's always full of spectators. I am compelled to take part in the deliberations, but I tremble with repugnance. Now, in any case, you will surely be invited to the meeting; if you behave today in accordance with my plan, the invitation will become an urgent request. But if, for some inconceivable reason, you're not invited after all, you will have to ask for an invitation; there's no doubt you'll get it then. So then, tomorrow you are sitting with the ladies in the governor's box. He looks upward again and again to make sure you're there. After various indifferent, ridiculous items on the agenda that are just sops for the audience — generally, harbor construction, always harbor construction! — the legal procedure comes up for discussion, too. If it isn't mentioned, or isn't mentioned soon enough, by the governor, I'll make sure that it gets mentioned. I'll stand up and make my report on today's execution. A very brief speech, nothing but the report. True, a report of that nature isn't customary, but I'll make it.

The governor thanks me, as always, with a friendly smile, and then he isn't able to restrain himself, he seizes the favorable opportunity. 'Just now,' he'll say, or words to that effect, 'the report on the execution has been made. I would merely like to add to this report the fact that the great explorer whose visit, which honors our colony so immensely, you all know about, was present at that very execution. Our meeting today is also made more significant by his presence. Now, shall we not ask this great explorer for his opinion of this old, traditional style of execution and of the proceedings that lead up to it?' Everyone naturally applauds to indicate approval and general consent, I loudest of all. The governor bows to you and says: 'Then, in the name of all assembled here, I pose the question.' And now you walk up to the railing. Place your hands where everyone can see them, or else the ladies will take hold of them and play with your fingers. — And now finally comes your speech. I don't know how I'll bear the suspense of the hours till then. In your talk you mustn't keep within any bounds; shout out the truth; lean over the railing; roar, yes, roar your opinion, your unalterable opinion, at the governor. But perhaps you don't want to, it doesn't suit your nature, perhaps in your country behavior in such situations is different; that's all right, too, even that is perfectly satisfactory; don't stand up at all, say only a few words, whisper them, so that only the officials right below you can hear; that's enough; you yourself don't need to speak about the lack of attendance at the execution, the squeaking cogwheel, the torn strap, the disgusting felt gag; no, I'll pick up on all the rest, and, trust me, if my speech doesn't actually drive him out of the room, at least it will bring him to his knees, so he'll have to avow: 'Old governor, I bow down before you.' — That's my plan; are you willing to help me carry it out? But of course you're willing; what's more, you must." And the officer grasped the explorer by both arms and looked him in the face, breathing heavily. He had shouted the last few sentences so loud that even the soldier and the condemned man had had their attention aroused; even though they couldn't understand any of it, still they stopped eating and looked over at the explorer as they chewed.

The answer he had to give was unequivocal for the explorer from the very outset; he had experienced too much in his life for him to possibly waver now; he was basically honest and he was fearless. Nevertheless he now hesitated for the space of a moment at the sight of the soldier and the condemned man. But finally he said as he had to: "No." The officer blinked his eyes several times, but didn't avert his gaze from him. "Do you want an explanation?" the explorer asked. The officer nodded in silence. "I'm an opponent of this procedure," the explorer now said; "even before you took me into your confidence — naturally, under no circumstances will I abuse that confidence — I had already considered whether I had any right to take steps against this procedure, and whether my intervention could have even a small chance of succeeding. It was clear to me whom I should turn to first if I wanted to do this: to the governor, of course. You made that even clearer to me, but you didn't plant the seeds of my decision; on the contrary, I sincerely respect your honest conviction, even if it can't lead me astray."

The officer remained silent, turned toward the machine, grasped one of the brass rods and then, bending backwards a little, looked up at the sketcher as if to check whether everything was in order. The soldier and the condemned man seemed to have become friends; difficult as it was to accomplish, being strapped in as tightly as he was, the condemned man made signs to the soldier; the soldier leaned over toward him; the condemned man whispered something to him, and the soldier nodded.

The explorer walked after the officer and said: "You still don't know what I intend to do. Yes, I'll give the governor my views about the procedure, but personally, not at an open meeting; furthermore, I won't be staying here long enough to be drawn into any meeting; by tomorrow morning I'll be sailing away or at least boarding the ship." It didn't look as if the officer had been listening. "So the procedure didn't win you over," he said to himself, and smiled, the way an old man smiles at a child's silliness while pursuing his own real thoughts behind the smile.

"Well, then, it's time," he finally said, and suddenly looked at the explorer with bright eyes that communicated some invitation, some summons to participate.

"Time for what?" asked the explorer uneasily, but received no reply.

"You're free," the officer said to the condemned man in the man's language. At first the man didn't believe it. "Well, you're free," said the officer. For the first time the condemned man's face showed real signs of life. Was it true? Was it only a caprice of the officer that might be only temporary? Had the foreign explorer won him a pardon? What was it? Those were the questions visible in his face. But not for long. Whatever the case might be, he wanted to be really free if he could, and he began to squirm, to the extent that the harrow would permit him to.

"You'll rip the straps on me," shouted the officer; "lie still! We're opening them now." And, along with the soldier, to whom he signaled, he set to work. The condemned man laughed quietly and wordlessly to himself; now he would turn his face to the officer on his left, now to the soldier on his right, nor did he forget the explorer.

"Pull him out," the officer ordered the soldier. To do this, some precautions had to be taken because of the harrow. As a result of his impatience the condemned man already had a few small scratches on his back. But, from this point on, the officer hardly gave him another thought. He walked up to the explorer, drew out the little leather wallet again, leafed through it, finally found the sheet he was looking for and showed it to the explorer. "Read it," he said. "I can't," said the explorer, "I've already told you I can't read these sheets." "But look at the sheet closely," said the officer, and stepped right next to the explorer to read along with him. When even that didn't help, he moved his little finger over the paper — but high above it, as if the sheet was in no case to be touched — in order to make it easier for the explorer to read. The explorer also made an effort, so that he could at least be obliging to the officer in this matter, but it was impossible. Now the officer began to spell out the inscription, and then he read it once more straight through. "It says 'Be just!' " he said, "now surely you can read it." The explorer bent so low over the paper that the officer moved it further away, fearing he might touch it; now the explorer said no more, but it was obvious that he still hadn't been able to read it. "It says 'Be just!' " the officer said again. "Could be," said the explorer, "I take your word for it." "Good," said the officer, at least partially contented, and, holding the sheet, stepped onto the ladder; with great care he inserted the sheet into the sketcher, apparently making a total rearrangement of the wheels; it was a very painstaking task; very small wheels must also have been involved; at times the officer's head disappeared in the sketcher altogether, because he had to examine the wheels so closely.

The explorer watched this labor from below without a pause; his neck grew stiff and his eyes hurt from the sunlight that streamed all over the sky. The soldier and the condemned man were occupied only with each other. The condemned man's shirt and trousers, which were already in the pit, were fished out by the soldier on the point of his bayonet. The shirt was horribly filthy, and the condemned man washed it in the bucket of water. When he then put on the shirt and trousers, both the soldier and the condemned man had to laugh out loud, because, after all, the garments were cut in two in the back. Perhaps the condemned man felt obligated to entertain the soldier; in his cut-up clothes he turned around in a circle in front of the soldier, who squatted on the ground and slapped his knees as he laughed. Nevertheless, they still controlled themselves out of regard for the gentlemen's presence.

When the officer was finally finished up above, he once more surveyed the whole thing in every detail, smiling all the while; now he closed the cover of the sketcher, which had been open up till then, climbed down, looked into the pit and then at the condemned man, noticed with satisfaction that he had taken his clothing out, then went to the bucket of water to wash his hands, realized too late how loathsomely filthy it now was, was sad about not being able to wash his hands, finally dipped them in the sand — he found this substitute inadequate but he had to make do with it — then stood up and started to unbutton his uniform jacket. As he did so, the two lady's handkerchiefs he had crammed behind his collar fell into his hands right away. "Here are your handkerchiefs for you," he said, throwing them to the condemned man. And to the explorer he said, by way of explanation, "Gifts from the ladies."

Despite the obvious haste with which he took off his jacket and then stripped completely, he nevertheless handled each garment very carefully; he even expressly ran his fingers over the silver braid on his jacket and shook a tassel back into place. It seemed inconsistent with this care, however, that, as soon as he was through handling a garment, he immediately threw it into the pit with an angry jerk. The last thing left to him was his short sword with its belt. He drew the sword from its sheath, broke it, then gathered everything together in his hand, the pieces of the sword, the sheath and the belt, and threw them away so violently that they clattered together down in the pit.

Now he stood there naked. The explorer bit his lips and said nothing. Of course, he knew what was going to happen, but he had no right to prevent the officer from doing anything he wanted. If the judicial procedure to which the officer was devoted was really so close to being abolished — possibly as a result of the intervention of the explorer, which the latter, for his part, felt obligated to go ahead with — then the officer was now acting perfectly correctly; in his place the explorer would have acted no differently.

At first the soldier and the condemned man understood nothing; at the beginning they didn't even watch. The condemned man was quite delighted to have gotten the handkerchiefs back, but he wasn't allowed to take pleasure in them long, because the soldier took them away from him in one rapid, unforeseeable grab. Now, in his turn, the condemned man tried to pull the handkerchiefs out of the belt under which he had stowed them, but the soldier was alert. They were fighting that way half-jokingly. Only when the officer was completely naked did they pay attention. The condemned man in particular seemed struck by the presentiment of some great shift in events. What had happened to him was now happening to the officer. Perhaps it would continue that way right up to the bitter end. Probably the foreign explorer had given the order for it. Thus it was revenge. Without having suffered all the way himself, he was nevertheless avenged all the way. A broad, soundless laugh now appeared on his face and no longer left it.

But the officer had turned toward the machine. If it had been clear even earlier that he understood the machine intimately, now it was absolutely astounding how he manipulated it and how it obeyed him. He had merely brought his hand close to the harrow and it rose and sank several times until reaching the proper position for receiving him; he merely clutched the bed by the edge and it already began to vibrate; the felt gag moved toward his mouth; it was evident that the officer didn't really want to use it, but his hesitation lasted only a moment; he gave in right away and closed his mouth around it. Everything was ready, only the straps still hung down along the sides, but they were obviously unnecessary; the officer didn't need to be buckled in. Then the condemned man noticed the loose straps; in his opinion the execution wouldn't be perfect if the straps weren't buckled tight; he made a vigorous sign to the soldier and they ran over to strap in the officer. He had already stretched out one foot to move the crank that was to set the sketcher in motion; then he saw that those two had come, so he pulled back his foot and let himself be strapped in. Now, of course, he could no longer reach the crank; neither the soldier nor the condemned man would be able to find it, and the explorer was determined not to move an inch. It wasn't necessary; the straps were scarcely in place when the machine started running; the bed vibrated, the needles danced on his skin; the harrow moved lightly up and down. The explorer had already been staring at the scene for some time before he recalled that a wheel in the sketcher should have been squeaking; but all was still, not the slightest whir was to be heard.

Because of this quietness, their attention was drawn away from the actual operation of the machine. The explorer looked over at the soldier and the condemned man. The condemned man was the livelier one; everything about the machine interested him; now he bent down, now he stretched upward; his index finger was constantly extended to show the soldier something. It was agonizing for the explorer. He was resolved to stay there to the end, but he knew he couldn't stand the sight of those two very long. "Go home," he said. The soldier may have been prepared to do so, but the condemned man looked on the order as an actual punishment. He asked beseechingly, with clasped hands, to be allowed to remain, and when the explorer shook his head and refused to give in, he even knelt down. The explorer saw that orders were of no use in this instance; he was about to go over and chase the two away. Then he heard a noise up in the sketcher. He looked up. Was that cogwheel creating a hindrance after all? But it was something else. Slowly the cover of the sketcher lifted and then flew wide open with a bang. The cog of a wheel became visible and rose higher, soon the whole wheel could be seen; it was as if some terrific force were compressing the sketcher, so that there was no more room for this wheel; the wheel turned until it reached the rim of the sketcher, fell down and rolled on its edge for some distance in the sand before coming to rest on its side. But up there a second wheel was already rising, followed by many more wheels, large, small and barely discernible ones; the same thing occurred with all of them; every time it seemed the sketcher surely had to be completely empty, a new, particularly numerous group appeared, rose, fell down, rolled in the sand and came to rest. This series of events made the condemned man completely forget the explorer's command; the cogwheels delighted him thoroughly; he kept trying to grab hold of one, at the same time spurring the soldier on to help him, but always drew back his hand in alarm, because that wheel was followed immediately by another wheel that frightened him, at least when it just started to roll.

The explorer, on the other hand, was very uneasy; the machine was obviously falling apart; the quietness of its operation was deceptive; he felt that he now had to do something for the officer, who could no longer take care of himself. But while the falling of the cogwheels had monopolized his entire attention, he had neglected to observe the rest of the machine; now, however, that the last cogwheel had left the sketcher and he bent over the harrow, he had a new, even worse surprise. The harrow wasn't writing, it was merely stabbing, and the bed wasn't turning the body over but merely lifting it, quivering, into the needles. The explorer wanted to intervene and possibly bring the whole thing to a standstill; this was no torture such as the officer wished to achieve, this was outright murder. He extended his hands. But at that moment the harrow was already lifting itself to the side with the skewered body, as it usually did only in the twelfth hour. The blood was flowing in a hundred streams, not mixed with water; the little water pipes had failed to work this time, as well. And now the final failure took place; the body didn't come loose from the long needles; it poured out its blood, but hung over the pit without falling. The harrow was already prepared to return to its former position, but, as if it noticed of its own accord that it was not yet free of its burden, it remained above the pit. "Why don't you help?" shouted the explorer to the soldier and the condemned man, seizing the officer's feet himself. He intended to press himself against the feet on this side, while those two grasped the officer's head on the other side, so he could be slowly removed from the needles. But now those two couldn't make up their minds to come; the condemned man actually turned away; the explorer had to go up to them and forcibly hustle them over to the officer's head. In doing so, he saw the face of the corpse, almost against his will. It was as it had been in life; no sign of the promised redemption could be discovered; what all the others had found in the machine, the officer did not find; his lips were tightly compressed, his eyes were open and had a living expression; his gaze was one of calm conviction; his forehead was pierced by the point of the big iron spike.

When the explorer, with the soldier and the condemned man behind him, arrived at the first houses of the colony, the soldier pointed to one and said: "Here is the teahouse."

On the ground floor of the house was a long, low, cavelike room, its walls and ceiling blackened by smoke. On the street side it was open for its entire width. Although the teahouse was not much different from the rest of the houses in the colony, which, except for the governor's palace complex, were all very rundown, it still gave the explorer the impression of a historic survival; and he felt the impact of earlier times. He stepped up closer and, followed by the two who were accompanying him, he walked among the unoccupied tables that stood in the street in front of the teahouse, inhaling the cool, musty air that came from inside. "The Old Man is buried here," said the soldier; "the priest refused to allow him a place in the cemetery. For a while people were undecided about where to bury him, finally they buried him here. I'm sure the officer didn't tell you anything about that, because he was naturally more ashamed of that than of anything else. He even tried a few times to dig the Old Man out at night, but he was always chased away." "Where is the grave?" asked the explorer, who couldn't believe the soldier. At once both of them, the soldier and the condemned man, ran ahead of him and with outstretched hands indicated a spot where they claimed the grave was located. They led the explorer all the way to the back wall, where customers were sitting at a few tables. Probably they were dock workers, powerful men with short beards that were so black they shone. All were jacketless, their shirts were torn, they were poor, downtrodden people. When the explorer approached, a few of them stood up, flattened themselves against the wall and looked in his direction. "It's a foreigner," was the whisper on all sides of the explorer; "he wants to see the grave." They pushed aside one of the tables, beneath which there actually was a gravestone. It was a simple stone, low enough to be concealed under a table. It bore an inscription in very small letters; the explorer had to kneel to read it. It said: "Here lies the old governor. His followers, who may not now reveal their names, dug this grave for him and erected the stone. There exists a prophecy that after a certain number of years the governor will rise again and will lead his followers out of this house to reconquer the colony. Believe and wait!" When the explorer had read this and stood up, he saw the men standing around him and smiling, as if they had read the inscription along with him, had found it ludicrous and were inviting him to share their opinion. The explorer acted as if he didn't notice this, distributed a few coins among them, waited until the table was pushed back over the grave, left the teahouse and went down to the harbor.

In the teahouse the soldier and the condemned man had run into acquaintances who detained them. But they must have torn themselves away from them quickly, because the explorer was still only halfway down the long flight of stairs that led to the boats when he saw they were already running after him. They probably wanted to force the explorer to take them along at the last moment. While the explorer, down below, was negotiating with a boatman to row him over to the steamer, those two dashed furiously down the steps, silently, because they didn't dare shout. But when they arrived down below, the explorer was already in the boat, which the boatman was just shoving off from shore. They might still have been able to jump into the boat, but the explorer picked up a heavy, knotted hawser from the floor, threatened them with it and thus prevented them from jumping.

A Country Doctor

I WAS IN a most awkward predicament: I needed to leave at once on an urgent journey; a seriously ill patient was waiting for me in a village ten miles away; a heavy snowstorm filled the wide interval between him and me; I had a carriage, light, with large wheels, perfectly suited to our country roads; wrapped in my fur coat, my instrument bag in my hand, I was already standing in the yard ready to go; but I lacked a horse, a horse. The previous night my own horse had died as a result of overwork in this glacial winter; my maid was now running all over the village trying to borrow a horse; but it was hopeless, I knew, and with more and more snow piling up on me, becoming more and more immobile, I stood there aimlessly. The maid showed up at the gate alone, swinging her lantern; naturally, who would lend his horse for such a ride? I walked across the yard once again; I could see no possibility; distracted, tormented, I kicked at the ramshackle door of the pigpen, which hadn't been used for years. It opened and swung back and forth on its hinges. Warmth and a smell like that of horses came out of it. A murky stable lantern was swinging by a rope inside. A man, crouching in the low shed, showed his candid, blue-eyed face. "Shall I hitch up?" he asked, creeping out on all fours. I could think of nothing to say, and only stooped down to see what else was in the pen. The maid stood next to me. "People don't know what they've got available in their own house," she said, and we both laughed. "Hey there, Brother! Hey there, Sister!" called the groom, and two horses, powerful animals with strong flanks, their legs drawn up tight to their bodies, lowering their well-formed heads like camels, slid out of the door one after the other solely by twisting their bodies to and fro, and occupied the doorway completely with not an inch to spare. But immediately they stood up on tall legs, their bodies steaming with dense vapor. "Help him," I said, and the willing maid ran to hand the groom the carriage harness. But the moment she has reached him, the groom embraces her and

76

shoves his face against hers. She yells out and escapes over to me; two rows of teeth have left their red marks on the girl's cheek. "You beast," I shout furiously, "would you like to feel my whip?" But I instantly recall that he's a stranger, that I don't know where he has come from, and that he's volunteering to help me when all the rest are failing me. As if he knew my thoughts, he isn't vexed by my threat, but still busy with the horses, merely turns once to face me. "Get in," he then says, and truly: everything is in readiness. I observe that I have never before handled such a beautiful team, and I get in cheerfully. "I'll do the driving, you don't know the way," I say. "Sure," he says, "I'm not going along at all, I'm staying with Rosa." "No!" yells Rosa and with a true foreboding that her fate is inevitable, she runs into the house; I hear the door chain rattle as she draws it tight; I hear the lock snap shut; I watch as, in addition, she turns off all the lights, first in the vestibule and then racing through the rooms, so she won't be found. "You're coming along," I say to the groom, "or I'm giving up the trip, no matter how urgent it is. I have no wish to hand the maid over to you as fare for the ride." "Giddy-up!" he says and claps his hands; the carriage is swept away like a piece of wood in a current; I can still hear the door of my house cracking and splintering as the groom assaults it, then my eyes and ears are filled with a rustling wind that penetrates all my senses uniformly. But even that lasts only a moment, because, as if my patient's farmyard opened up directly in front of the gate of my own yard, I am already there; the horses are standing calmly; the snowfall has ended; moonlight all around; the parents of the patient rush out of the house; his sister after them; they practically lift me out of the carriage; I can't make out any of their confused talk; in the sickroom the air is barely breathable; the stove, which hadn't been tended to, is smoking. I intend to open the window; but first I want to see the patient. Then, with no fever, not cold, not warm, with expressionless eyes, without a shirt, the boy raises himself up under the feather bed, embraces my neck and whispers in my ear: "Doctor, let me die." I look around; no one has heard; his parents are standing in silence, bending forward in expectation of my medical opinion; the sister has brought a chair for my bag. I open the bag and look through my instruments; the boy continues to grope toward me from his bed in order to remind me of his request; I take hold of some tweezers, examine them in the candlelight and put them down again. "Yes," I think blasphemously, "in such cases, the gods come to your aid; they send the missing horse; because of the urgency, they add a second one; and in their bounty they then grant you the groom — " It is only then that I think of Rosa again; what am I to do, how can I rescue her, how can I pull her out from under that groom when I am ten miles away from her and unmanageable horses are harnessed to my carriage? Those horses, which somehow have now loosened the reins and in some unknown way have opened the windows from outside! Each one has thrust its head in through a window and, heedless of the family's outcry, is scrutinizing the patient. "I'll ride right back," I think, as if the horses are inviting me to go, but I allow the sister, who believes I am numb from the heat, to take off my fur coat. A glass of rum is prepared for me, the old man pats me on the shoulder; the surrender of this treasure of his justifies that familiarity. I shake my head; I would grow ill within the old man's circumscribed way of thinking; for that reason alone, I refuse the drink. The mother stands by the bed and entices me over; I obey and, while a horse neighs loudly at the ceiling, I place my head on the chest of the boy, who shivers at the touch of my wet beard. What I know is confirmed: the boy is healthy, with somewhat poor circulation, glutted with coffee* by his anxious mother, but healthy, so that the best thing would be to shove him out of bed. But I'm not out to improve the world, and I let him lie there. I'm an employee of the district government and I do my duty to the hilt, to the point where it's almost too much. Though badly paid, I'm generous and helpful to the poor. I still must take care of Rosa, then the boy may be right and I, too, shall die. What am I doing here in this endless winter? My horse is dead, and there's no one in the village who'll lend me his. I have to find my team in the pigpen; if, by chance, they weren't horses, I'd have to drive with sows. That's the way it is. And I nod at the family. They know nothing about it, and if they knew, they wouldn't believe it. Writing prescriptions is easy, but, otherwise, communicating with people is hard. Well, this seems to be the end of my call here, once again I've been annoyed for nothing; I'm used to that, with the help of my night bell the whole district tortures me; but having to give up Rosa, too, this time, that beautiful girl who has lived in my house for years, and whom I scarcely noticed — that sacrifice is too great, and I must somehow square it temporarily in my own mind through sophistries if I'm not to make an all-out attack on this family, because, even with the best will in the world, they can't give me back Rosa. But as I am closing my bag and signaling to have my coat brought over, as the family stands there together, the father sniffing at the glass of rum in his hand, the mother, whom I have most likely disappointed — what do the people expect of me? — biting her lips tearfully, and the sister waving a blood-soaked towel, I am somehow ready to admit on certain conditions that the boy is perhaps ill after all. I go over to him, he smiles at me as I approach as if I were bringing him, say, the most invigorating

---

* [Untranslatable wordplay here: for "with . . . circulation" the German has *durchblutet*; for "glutted," *durchtränkt*. — TRANS.]

soup — oh, now both horses are neighing; the noise, ordained by some lofty powers, is probably meant to facilitate my examination — and I find: yes, the boy is ill. On his right side, around the hip, a wound as large as the palm of one's hand has opened up. Pink,* in many shades, dark as it gets deeper, becoming light at the edges, softly granular, with irregular accumulations of blood, wide open as the surface entrance to a mine. That's how it looks from some distance. But, close up, a complication can be seen, as well. Who can look at it without giving a low whistle? Worms as long and thick as my little finger, naturally rose-colored and in addition spattered with blood, firmly attached to the inside of the wound, with white heads and many legs, are writhing upward into the light. Poor boy, there's no hope for you. I have discovered your great wound; you will be destroyed by this flower on your side. The family is happy; it sees me active; the sister tells it to the mother, the mother to the father, the father to a few guests who are entering the open door through the moonlight on tiptoe, balancing with outstretched arms. "Will you save me?" the boy whispers with a sob, completely dazzled by the life in his wound. That's how the people are in my area. Always asking the doctor for the impossible. They've lost their old faith; the priests sits home and picks his vestments to pieces, one after another; but the doctor is supposed to accomplish everything with his gentle, surgical hands. Well, have it any way you like: I didn't offer my services; if you misuse me for religious purposes, I'll go along with that, too; what better can I ask for, an old country doctor, robbed of my maid! And they come, the family and the village elders, and they undress me; a school choir led by their teacher is standing in front of the house and singing an extremely simple setting of these words:

> Undress him, then he will cure,
> And if he doesn't cure, then kill him!
> It's only a doctor, it's only a doctor.

Then I'm undressed and, my fingers in my beard, I look at the people calmly with head bowed. I am completely composed and superior to them all, and remain so, too, even though it doesn't help me, because now they take me by the head and feet and carry me into the bed. They lay me against the wall, on the side where the wound is. Then they all leave the room; the door is closed; the singing dies away; clouds pass in front of the moon; the bedclothes lie warmly on top of me, the horses' heads in the window openings waver like shadows. "Do you know,"

---

* [In German, *Rosa*. A wordplay? — TRANS.]

I hear, spoken into my ear, "I don't have much confidence in *you*. You just drifted in here from somewhere, you didn't come on your own two feet. Instead of helping, you're just crowding me out of my deathbed. I'd like most of all to scratch your eyes out." "Right," I say, "it's a disgrace. But I'm a doctor, you see. What should I do? Believe me, it's not easy for me, either." "Am I supposed to be contented with that excuse? Oh, I guess I must, I'm always forced to be contented. I came into the world with a fine wound; that was my entire portion in life." "My young friend," I say, "your mistake is this: you don't have the big picture. I, who have already been in all sickrooms, far and wide, tell you: your wound isn't that bad. Brought on by two hatchet blows at an acute angle. Many people offer their sides and scarcely hear the hatchet in the forest, let alone having it come closer to them." "Is it really so, or are you fooling me in my fever?" "It's really so, take a government doctor's word of honor into the next world with you." And he took it, and fell silent. But now it was time to think about how to save myself. The horses still stood faithfully in their places. Clothing, fur coat and bag were quickly seized and bundled together; I didn't want to waste time getting dressed; if the horses made the same good time as on the way over, I would, so to speak, be jumping out of this bed into mine. Obediently a horse withdrew from the window; I threw the bundle into the carriage; the fur coat flew too far, it just barely caught on to a hook with one sleeve. Good enough. I leaped onto the horse. The reins loosely trailing along, one horse just barely attached to the other, the carriage meandering behind, the fur coat bringing up the rear in the snow. "Giddy-up, and look lively," I said, but the ride wasn't lively; as slowly as old men we proceeded across the snowy waste; for a long time there resounded behind us the new, but incorrect, song of the children:

> Rejoice, O patients,
> The doctor has been put in bed alongside you!

Traveling this way, I'll never arrive home; my flourishing practice is lost; a successor is robbing me, but it will do him no good, because he can't replace me; in my house the loathsome groom is rampaging; Rosa is his victim; I don't want to think of all the consequences. Naked, exposed to the frost of this most unhappy era, with an earthly carriage and unearthly horses, I, an old man, roam about aimlessly. My fur coat is hanging in back of the carriage, but I can't reach it, and no one among the sprightly rabble of my patients lifts a finger to help. Betrayed! Betrayed! Having obeyed the false ringing of the night bell just once — the mistake can never be rectified.

A Report to an Academy

You have honored me with your invitation to submit a report to the Academy about my former life as an ape.

Taking this invitation in its literal sense, I am unfortunately unable to comply with it. Nearly five years stand between me and my apehood, a period that may be short in terms of the calendar but is an infinitely long one to gallop through as I have done, accompanied for certain stretches by excellent people, advice, applause and band music, but fundamentally on my own, because, to remain within the metaphor, all that accompaniment never got very close to the rail. This achievement would have been impossible if I had willfully clung to my origins, to the memories of my youth. In fact, avoidance of all willfulness was the supreme commandment I had imposed on myself; I, a free ape, accepted that yoke. Thereby, however, my memories were in turn increasingly lost to me. If at first a return to the past, should the humans have so wished, was as wide open to me as the universal archway the sky forms over the earth, at the same time my wildly accelerated development made this archway increasingly low and narrow; I felt more at ease and sheltered in the human world; the storm winds that blew out of my past grew calm; today there is only a breeze that cools my heels; and the hole in the distance through which it issues, and from which I once issued, has become so small that, if I ever had sufficient strength and desire to run all the way back there, I would have to scrape the hide off my body to squeeze through. Speaking frankly (although I enjoy using figures of speech for these matters), speaking frankly: your own apehood, gentlemen, to the extent that there is anything like that in your past, cannot be more remote from you than mine is from me. But every wanderer on earth feels a tickling in his heels: the little chimpanzee and great Achilles. In the most limited sense, however, I may be able to satisfy your

81

demands, and, in fact, I do so with great pleasure. The first thing I learned was shaking hands; shaking hands indicates candidness; today, when I am at the pinnacle of my career, why not add my candid words to that first handshake? My report will not teach the Academy anything basically new and will fall far short of what has been asked of me, which, with the best will in the world, I am unable to tell you — nevertheless, it is meant to show the guidelines by which a former ape has burst into the human world and established himself there. But I certainly would not have the right to make even the insignificant statement that follows, if I were not completely sure of myself and had not secured a truly unassailable position on all the great vaudeville stages of the civilized world.

I come from the Gold Coast. For the story of how I was captured I must rely on the reports of others. A hunting expedition of the Hagenbeck* firm — incidentally, since then I've drained many a fine bottle of red wine with its leader — was lying in wait in the brush by the shore when I ran down to the watering place one evening in the midst of a pack of apes. They fired; I was the only one hit; I was wounded in two places.

One wound was in the cheek; that was slight, but left behind a large, red, hairless scar, which won me the repulsive, totally unsuitable name of Red Peter, which must have been invented by an ape! — as if the red spot on my cheek were the only difference between me and the trained ape Peter, who had a local reputation here and there and who kicked the bucket recently. But that's by the by.

The second bullet hit me below the hip. It was a serious wound and the cause of my limping a little even today. Not long ago I read in an article by one of the ten thousand windbags† who gab about me in the papers, saying my ape nature is not yet suppressed; the proof being that, when visitors come, I'm fond of taking off my trousers to show where the bullet hit me. That guy should have every last finger of the hand he writes with individually blasted off! *I, I* have the right to drop my pants in front of anyone I feel like; all they'll see there is a well-tended coat of fur and the scar left over from — here let us choose a specific word for a specific purpose, but a word I wouldn't want misunderstood — the scar left over from an infamous shot. Everything is open and aboveboard; there's nothing to hide; when it comes to the truth, every high-minded person rejects namby-pamby etiquette. On the other hand, if that writer were to take his trousers off when company came, you can be sure it

* [Carl Hagenbeck of Hamburg was a pioneering zoo director, circus entrepreneur and supplier of live animals for exhibitions of all kinds. — TRANS.]

† [One of Kafka's animal jokes is irretrievably lost in translation here: the word he uses for "windbags" also means "greyhounds." — TRANS.]

would look quite different, and I'm ready to accept it as a token of his good sense that he refrains from doing so. But then he shouldn't bedevil me with his delicate sensibilities!

After those shots I woke up — and here my own recollections gradually begin — in a cage between decks on the Hagenbeck steamer. It wasn't a four-sided cage with bars all around; instead, there were only three barred sides attached to a crate, so that the crate formed the fourth wall. The whole thing was too low for standing erect in, and too narrow for sitting down in. And so I squatted with bent, constantly trembling knees, and, since at first I probably didn't want to see anyone and felt like being in the dark all the time, I faced the crate, while behind me the bars cut into my flesh. This way of keeping wild animals right after their capture is considered advantageous, and, with the experience I have today, I can't deny that, in a human sense, it is really the case.

But at that time I didn't think about it. For the first time in my life I had no way out, or at least not straight ahead of me; right in front of me was the crate, each board tightly joined to the next. True, between the boards there was a gap running right through, and when I first discovered it I greeted it with a joyful howl of ignorance, but this gap wasn't even nearly wide enough for me to push my tail through,* and all my ape's strength couldn't widen it.

They told me later on that I made unusually little noise, from which they concluded that I would either go under, or else, if I managed to live through the first, critical period, I would be extremely trainable. I lived through that period. Muffled sobbing, painful searching for fleas, weary licking of a coconut, banging the side of the crate with my cranium, sticking out my tongue whenever someone approached — those were my first occupations in my new life. But, throughout it all, only that one feeling: no way out. Today, naturally, I can only sketch from hindsight, and in human words, what I then felt as an ape, and therefore I am sketching it incorrectly, but even if I can no longer attain the old apish truth, my description isn't basically off course, and no doubt about it.

And yet, up to then, I had had so many ways out and now no longer one. I had boxed myself in. If I had been nailed down that couldn't have subtracted from my freedom of action. Why so? Scratch the skin between your toes till it bleeds, and you still won't find the reason. Press yourself backwards against the bars until they nearly cut you in two, you

---

* [There are several indications in the story, and in posthumously published deleted fragments, that Kafka meant Red Peter to be a chimpanzee; he either didn't know or didn't care that chimpanzees have no tail. (The German *Affe* that Kafka mainly uses means either ape or monkey indiscriminately.) — TRANS.]

won't find the reason. I had no way out, but had to create one for myself, because without it I couldn't live. Always up against the side of that crate — I would definitely have dropped dead. But, for Hagenbeck, apes belong at the side of the crate — so I stopped being an ape. A lucid, elegant train of thought, which I must have somehow hatched out with my belly, because apes think with their belly.

I'm afraid that it may not be clearly understood what I mean by "a way out." I am using the phrase in its most common and most comprehensive sense. I purposely do not say "freedom." I don't mean that expansive feeling of freedom on all sides. As an ape I might have known it, and I've met human beings who long for it. As for me, however, I didn't desire freedom then, and I don't now. Incidentally: human beings fool themselves all too often on the subject of freedom. And just as freedom counts among the loftiest feelings, so does the corresponding delusion count among the loftiest. Often in vaudeville houses, before my act came on, I've seen some pair of artists do their trapeze routine way up near the ceiling. They swung to and fro, they rocked back and forth, they made leaps, they floated into each other's arms, one held the other by the hair with his teeth. "That, too, is human freedom," I would muse, "movement achieved in sovereign self-confidence." You mockery of holy Nature! No building would remain unshaken by the laughter of the ape world at that sight.

No, it wasn't freedom I wanted. Only a way out; to the right, to the left, in any direction at all; I made no other demands; even if the way out were a delusion; the demand was a small one, the delusion wouldn't be any bigger. To move forward, to move forward! Anything but standing still with raised arms, flattened against the side of a crate.

Today I see it clearly: without the utmost inner calm I would never have been able to save myself. And, in reality, I may owe everything that I've achieved to the calm that came over me after the first few days there on the ship. But, in turn, I probably owe that calm to the people on the ship.

They're good sorts, despite everything. Even today I enjoy recalling the sound of their heavy steps, which at the time reechoed in my half-slumber. They had the habit of tackling everything as slowly as possible. If one of them wanted to rub his eyes, he would lift his hand as if it were a hanging weight. Their jokes were coarse but hearty. Their laughter was always mingled with a coughing sound that sounded dangerous but was insignificant. They always had something in their mouth they could spit out and they didn't care a bit where they spat it. They were always complaining that my fleas were jumping onto them; but they were never seriously mad at me for it; they were perfectly well aware that fleas thrive in my fur and that fleas jump; they reconciled themselves to it. When they had no duties, sometimes a few of them would sit down in a semicircle around me; they rarely spoke but just mumbled to one another like pigeons cooing; they would stretch out on crates and smoke their pipes; they would slap their knees the minute I made the slightest movement; and from time to time one of them would take a stick and tickle me where I liked it. If I were to be invited today to take part in a voyage on that ship, I would certainly decline the invitation, but it is equally certain that the memories I could muse over from my days between the decks there are not all unpleasant.

The calm I acquired in the company of those people restrained me especially from any attempt to escape. From the vantage point of today, it seems to me I had at least a vague notion that I had to find a way out if I were to survive, but that the way out was not to be attained by escape. I no longer know for certain whether escape was possible, but I think so; an ape probably always has some means of escape. With my teeth as they are today, I have to be careful even when cracking an ordinary nut, but at the time I would probably certainly have managed to bite through the lock on the door in a matter of time. I didn't. What would I have gained if I had? They would have caught me again the minute I stuck my head out and locked me in a cage that was worse yet; or else I might have escaped unnoticed and run over to other animals, for instance the giant snakes opposite me, and breathed my last in their embraces; or I might even have successfully stolen away onto the top deck and jumped overboard; in that case, I would have rocked on the ocean for a while and then drowned. Deeds of desperation. My calculations weren't that human, but under the influence of my environment I behaved as if I had calculated it all.

I didn't calculate, but I did observe things very calmly. I watched those human beings walk back and forth, always the same faces, the same motions; it often seemed to me as if it was just a single person. Well, that person or those persons were walking around unmolested. A lofty goal hazily entered my mind. Nobody promised me that, if I became like them, the bars would be removed. Promises like that based on apparently impossible terms just aren't made. But if the terms are met, later on the promises turn up exactly where they were formerly sought in vain. Now, there was nothing about these humans in themselves that allured me all that much. If I were a devotee of that above-mentioned freedom, I would certainly have chosen the ocean over the kind of way out that offered itself to me in the dull eyes of those people. At any rate, I had already been observing them long before I thought about such things; in fact, it was the accumulation of observations that first pushed me in the chosen direction.

It was so easy to imitate people. I could already spit within the first few days. Then we would mutually spit in each other's faces; the only difference being that I licked my face clean afterwards, and they didn't. I was soon smoking a pipe like an old hand; if, when doing so, I still stuck my thumb into the bowl, everyone between the decks whooped with joy; it was only the difference between the empty and filled pipe that I didn't understand for a long time.

It was the liquor bottle that gave me most trouble. The smell was torture to me; I forced myself with all my strength; but weeks went by before I overcame the resistance. Oddly, it was these inward struggles that the people took more seriously than anything else about me. Although in my recollections I can't tell the people apart, there was one of them who came again and again, alone or with comrades, by day and night, at the most varied hours; he would place himself in front of me with the bottle and give me instruction. He couldn't comprehend me, he wanted to solve the riddle of my being. Slowly he uncorked the bottle and then looked at me to see if I had understood; I confess, I always watched him with frantic, exaggerated attention; no human teacher will ever find such a human pupil anywhere on earth; after the bottle was uncorked, he lifted it to his mouth; my eyes followed him all the way into his gullet; he nodded, contented with me, and put the bottle to his lips; I, delighted by dawning knowledge, then squeal and scratch myself all over wherever I feel the need; he is happy, presses the bottle against his mouth and takes a swallow; I, impatient and desperate to emulate him, soil myself in my cage, and this, too, gives him great satisfaction; and now, holding the bottle far away from himself and lifting it toward himself again briskly, he bends backwards with pedagogical exaggeration and empties it in one draught. I, worn out by the excess of my desire, am unable to follow any longer and hang weakly on the bars while he concludes the theoretical instruction by rubbing his stomach and grinning.

Only now does the practical exercise begin. Am I not too exhausted already by the theoretical part? Far too exhausted, most likely. That's how my destiny goes. All the same, I do the best I can as I reach for the bottle he holds out to me; trembling, I uncork it; as I succeed, I gradually acquire new strength; I lift the bottle, by this time imitating my model so closely that there's hardly any difference; I put it to my mouth and — and with loathing, with loathing, even though it's empty and only the smell is left, with loathing I throw it on the ground. To my teacher's sorrow, to my own greater sorrow; I fail to make things right with either him or myself when, even after throwing away the bottle, I don't forget to do an excellent job of rubbing my stomach and grinning at the same time.

Things went that way all too often during my course of instruction. And to my teacher's credit: he wasn't angry with me; true, he sometimes held his lit pipe against my fur until it started to get singed in some spot that was very hard to reach, but then he would put it out again himself with his gigantic, kindly hand; he wasn't angry with me, he realized that we were both fighting as allies against ape nature, and the difficulty was more on my side.

What a victory it was, then, for him and for me, when one evening, before a large group of spectators — maybe it was a party, a gramophone was playing, an officer was walking about among the men — when on that evening, while no one was observing me, I grasped a liquor bottle that had been accidentally left in front of my cage, uncorked it according to all the rules as the people paid increasingly greater attention, put it to my mouth and, without hesitating, without twisting my lips, like a drinker from way back, with rolling eyes and gurgling throat, really and truly emptied the bottle; threw it away, no longer like someone in despair, but like an artiste; did actually forget to rub my stomach; but, instead, because I simply had to, because I had the urge to, because my senses were in an uproar — in a word, I called out "Hello," breaking into human speech, leaping into the human community by means of that outcry, and feeling its echo, "Listen, he's talking," like a kiss all over my sweat-soaked body.

I repeat: I didn't imitate human beings because they appealed to me; I imitated because I was looking for a way out, for no other reason. And that victory still didn't amount to much. My speaking voice failed me again immediately, and it took months for it to come back; my aversion to the liquor bottle returned and was even stronger than before. But, all the same, my course was set once and for all.

When I was handed over to the first trainer in Hamburg, I immediately recognized the two possibilities that were open to me: zoo or vaudeville. I didn't hesitate. I told myself: make every effort to get into vaudeville; that's the way out; the zoo is just another cage; once you land there, you're lost.

And I learned, gentlemen. Oh, you learn when you have to; you learn when you want a way out; you learn regardless of all else. You observe yourself, whip in hand; you lacerate yourself at the least sign of resistance. My ape nature, turning somersaults, raged out of me and away, so that my first teacher nearly became apelike himself, and soon had to give up the instruction and go to a sanatorium. Fortunately he came out again before long.

But I used up many teachers, sometimes a few teachers simultaneously. When I had become more sure of my abilities, when the public was following my progress and my future began to look bright, I took on teachers on my own, sat them down in five successive rooms and took lessons from all of them at once, uninterruptedly leaping from one room to another.

That progress! That penetration of rays of knowledge from all sides into my awakening brain! I won't deny it: it made me happy. But I also admit: I didn't overestimate it, not even then, let alone today. Through an effort that hasn't found its match on earth to the present day, I have attained the educational level of an average European. Perhaps that wouldn't be anything by itself, but it is really something when you consider that it helped me out of my cage and gave me this particular way out, this human way out. There's an excellent German expression: *sich in die Büsche schlagen,** to steal away secretly. That's what I did, I stole away secretly. I had no other way, always presupposing that I couldn't choose freedom.

When I survey my development and the goal it has had up to now, I am neither unhappy nor contented. My hands in my trousers pockets, the wine bottle on the table, I half recline, half sit, in my rocking chair and look out the window. When a visitor comes, I receive him in a proper manner. My impresario sits in the anteroom; when I ring, he comes and listens to what I have to say. There's a performance almost every evening, and my success probably can't get much greater. When I come home late at night from banquets, learned societies or friendly gatherings, a little half-trained female chimpanzee is waiting for me and I have a good time with her, ape fashion; in the daytime I don't want to see her, because her eyes have that deranged look which bewildered trained animals have; I'm the only one who recognizes it, and I can't stand it.

All in all, however, I have achieved what I wanted to achieve. Let nobody say that it wasn't worth the trouble. Anyway, I don't want any human being's opinion, I merely wish to disseminate information; I am merely making a report; even to you, gentlemen of the Academy, I have merely made a report.

DOVER · THRIFT · EDITIONS

FICTION

THE QUEEN OF SPADES AND OTHER STORIES, Alexander Pushkin. 128pp. 0-486-28054-3

THE STORY OF AN AFRICAN FARM, Olive Schreiner. 256pp. 0-486-40165-0

FRANKENSTEIN, Mary Shelley. 176pp. 0-486-28211-2

THE JUNGLE, Upton Sinclair. 320pp. (Available in U.S. only.) 0-486-41923-1

THREE LIVES, Gertrude Stein. 176pp. (Available in U.S. only.) 0-486-28059-4

THE BODY SNATCHER AND OTHER TALES, Robert Louis Stevenson. 80pp. 0-486-41924-X

THE STRANGE CASE OF DR. JEKYLL AND MR. HYDE, Robert Louis Stevenson. 64pp. 0-486-26688-5

TREASURE ISLAND, Robert Louis Stevenson. 160pp. 0-486-27559-0

GULLIVER'S TRAVELS, Jonathan Swift. 240pp. 0-486-29273-8

THE KREUTZER SONATA AND OTHER SHORT STORIES, Leo Tolstoy. 144pp. 0-486-27805-0

THE WARDEN, Anthony Trollope. 176pp. 0-486-40076-X

FATHERS AND SONS, Ivan Turgenev. 176pp. 0-486-40073-5

ADVENTURES OF HUCKLEBERRY FINN, Mark Twain. 224pp. 0-486-28061-6

THE ADVENTURES OF TOM SAWYER, Mark Twain. 192pp. 0-486-40077-8

THE MYSTERIOUS STRANGER AND OTHER STORIES, Mark Twain. 128pp. 0-486-27069-6

HUMOROUS STORIES AND SKETCHES, Mark Twain. 80pp. 0-486-29279-7

AROUND THE WORLD IN EIGHTY DAYS, Jules Verne. 160pp. 0-486-41111-7

CANDIDE, Voltaire (François-Marie Arouet). 112pp. 0-486-26689-3

GREAT SHORT STORIES BY AMERICAN WOMEN, Candace Ward (ed.). 192pp. 0-486-28776-9

"THE COUNTRY OF THE BLIND" AND OTHER SCIENCE-FICTION STORIES, H. G. Wells. 160pp. (Not available in Europe or United Kingdom.) 0-486-29569-9

THE ISLAND OF DR. MOREAU, H. G. Wells. 112pp. (Not available in Europe or United Kingdom.) 0-486-29027-1

THE INVISIBLE MAN, H. G. Wells. 112pp. (Not available in Europe or United Kingdom.) 0-486-27071-8

THE TIME MACHINE, H. G. Wells. 80pp. (Not available in Europe or United Kingdom.) 0-486-28472-7

THE WAR OF THE WORLDS, H. G. Wells. 160pp. (Not available in Europe or United Kingdom.) 0-486-29506-0

ETHAN FROME, Edith Wharton. 96pp. 0-486-26690-7

SHORT STORIES, Edith Wharton. 128pp. 0-486-28235-X

THE AGE OF INNOCENCE, Edith Wharton. 288pp. 0-486-29803-5

THE PICTURE OF DORIAN GRAY, Oscar Wilde. 192pp. 0-486-27807-7

JACOB'S ROOM, Virginia Woolf. 144pp. (Not available in Europe or United Kingdom.) 0-486-40109-X